ENI

"Reading this book I felt I was right t... ... the middle of this gripping story." -- *Joanna Haverkamp, Lead Pastor Hillsong Germany*

"Nancy Lueckhof vividly recounts a true tale that exposes her readers to a culture very different from their own. Life with her family among the Filipino people adds depth and dimension to her storytelling. Characters come to life in this coming of age account. A debut novel that's a page-turner by an author who's lived the adventure."
Ron Tucker, Senior Pastor Grace Church, St. Louis, Missouri

"SULUAN takes the soul through a tempestuous journey like none other. The devastating tropical storm setting perfectly mirrors the inner world of teenager Antonia, who is shredded by her horrific passage from carefree youth into young adulthood. Lueckhof's illustrative style creates an unforgettable cinematic experience for the senses and a poignant challenge for the mind and spirit. Caution: readers should buckle their seat-belts for an emotional roller coaster adventure of a lifetime!"
Claudia Porter, Author, Teacher, Pastor
Torchgrab Ministries, Denver, Colorado

"Having known Nancy as friend, colleague, and community-aid worker, but not as author, my reaction to my wife upon reading SULUAN was, "Wow! This girl can write!" And nothing over the ensuing pages changed my mind. Perhaps Nancy didn't eat or even snack as she was writing. For as she says at the beginning of her first novel, SULUAN, "As hunger is the best cook, so too are adventure and tragedy the best ingredients for a

storyteller." This book has it all: adventure, tragedy, romance, and a miracle that, even once you've read it, will have you shaking your head in wonder. The only thing is, this miracle is somehow true."
Peter Steike, Pastor, Motivational Speaker
Home Church Equipper, Adelaide, Australia

"SULUAN is the most powerful story I have ever read. I wept through the whole thing. This is a masterpiece. May God give favor and open doors to give this story the widest possible distribution. I'm thinking: big-budget movie!"
David McIntire, Author of "The Rafter Book", Maui, Hawaii

"Only Nancy could've captured the true heart and story of SULUAN. Having lived and worked among the beautiful Filipinos for many years, her attention to detail in this dazzling and riveting adventure will draw you in, making you feel like you are right there in the Philippines!"
Jill LeBlanc, Singer/Songwriter, Minister, Author and Speaker
www.CharlieandJill.com

"SULUAN is such a book, that once you've begun to read it, you cannot put it down. Nancy Lueckhof has invested her whole heart into the story, and every bit of her investment was well worth it. Anyone who reads SULUAN will feel her passion and see even the smallest detail described with great beauty. We are pleased to count Nancy as one of our friends. She is a richly talented woman; her abilities as a writer are credible and authentic. Whoever writes as well as she does, surely will be writing more. We are eager to see what Nancy will publish next!"
Martin Seiler, Pastor Gospel Forum-Stuttgart, Royal Ranger Scouts Regional Leader, Germany

SULUAN

A Novel by Nancy Lueckhof

WiseHeart
Publications

Published by WiseHeart Publications

The Library of Congress has catalogued the trade paperback original
edition of this book as follows:

Lueckhof, Nancy, 1957—
Suluan

Pages 247 cm 13.335 x 20.32

Original cover design copyright © 2014 by Benjamin Lueckhof
Cover photograph by Felix Eichhorn
Mini Shark Logo copyright © 2014 by Benjamin Lueckhof
Photo of Wave Stock 1 by RaeyenIrael-Stock
Cover model - Mellenie Rose Ylanan, Inayawan, Cebu
Suluan photographs by Friederich Lueckhof
Photo of author by Benjamin Lueckhof

All Rights Reserved

ISBN-10: 099096910X
ISBN-13: 978-0-9909691-0-5

1.   Historical Fiction—Adventure—Typhoon—Philippines—
Whale Shark—Island Life   I. Title.

2014955777

DEDICATION

To all the precious people who live on Suluan.
This is your story. May this amazing tale
be a constant reminder of God's love, care,
and His interest in your beautiful island.

. . .

To Pastor Narciso (Jhun) Sayson, Jr., who shared
not only the details of his mother's miraculous rescue
but also the infectious love that he has
for her home place, Suluan.
May this book serve as a testimony of God's work
in the life of your entire family.

. . .

To our staff and all the precious Pro.Vision Kids.
May the courage of Antonia Arceno infuse you with hope
to trust in a BIG, miraculous God!

. . .

To my Lord and Savior, Jesus Christ.
May all who read this account of Antonia's life
see Your mighty hand of salvation, provision,
and complete restoration.

CONTENTS

ACKNOWLEDGMENTS

To my husband, Friederich, for choosing me
as your wife, and for inviting me to join you
in your work here on these beautiful islands.
I love you. *It's more fun in the Philippines!*

To my son, Benjamin, for your brilliant designs,
your tireless patience with me, and your superb creative
skills. I am honored to be your mom.

To Dr. S. Anna Stepanek, Ph.D., my incredible sister,
who believed that I really *could* write a novel. Love you!

To Josua Nilkens, for the creative lyrics and
inspiration on your beautiful "You Give Me Hope" CD.

To Hans and Ingrid Gass, who opened their home
in Èpinouze, France to allow me to write the bulk of this
story in an atmosphere of beauty and peace.

To Sarah Haas and David McIntire for the kindness of
your excellent input and eagle-eye editing expertise.

PREFACE

Seasick? Absolutely! Up and down, up and down, over the rowdy Pacific waters I rocked for eight, *count 'em*, eight long, grueling hours on my way to the island of Suluan in the spring of 2006. Even just *thinking* about it now, I feel queasy.

I almost drowned as a child, so traveling in water where I cannot see the bottom is *not* my idea of a fun trip, nor is being caught in a wicked storm at sea.

But here I was, no land in sight, at the ends of the earth, rumbling and bouncing along over the deep waters in a motorized Filipino pump boat. Did I think about sharks? *Of course I did!*

I recall how my mind swam with a *true story* that I had just heard before that trip -- about a teenage girl from Suluan who had been lost at sea alone for almost two weeks. *And she survived!*

The tale of *how* she survived captured my imagination and grabbed my curiosity. The events of the tragedy and shocking details of her rescue sounded like something straight out of an ancient legend or a Walt Disney box-office hit.

SULUAN is based on as many true facts as I could research and gather directly from the son of Antonia, the heroine of this novel, as well as countless other historical details about the Philippines in the 1930s.

Over the ensuing years, I visited the island of Suluan many times. Each time I fell more in love with the beauty and simplicity I found there.

That is why the book begins high on the cliffs and inside a mysterious secret cave. Using details and imagery, I want to introduce you to the sights, sounds, and smells of an old and ancient world *before* the stressful adventure at sea begins.

My hope is that you fall in love with the Philippines and her people as I have. My prayer is that you will be inspired by the lives of these characters. And, that you can wrap your mind around an incredible story that begged to be written down and passed on to others.

The beauty of the Philippines is indeed her people and their "bounce-back" spirit and strength.

Thank God for Dramamine,
Nancy Lueckhof

CHAPTER ONE
THE CAVE ON THE CLIFFS

The snaggletoothed cave sat high atop the cliffs, with a 200-foot drop-down past jagged rocks to a relentless pounding surf. The precipice was entirely off-limits to the teens on Suluan. Although the parents in the small village frequently warned the youths to stay away, they still feared their children falling off the dangerous rocky overhang and into the sea.

But their worries didn't begin or end with the cliffs. They nurtured gnawing fears that their children might someday die in a tragic accident or vanish forever far from home. Superstition gripped the remote Philippine island.

Age-old stories of unexplained happenings near this cave were as numerous as the coconuts that hung in the nearby trees. These were tales of the bizarre -- passed down in exaggerated detail from generation to generation and shared among the villagers on the island of Suluan.

They were stories of the "Wok-Wok" in magic trees, of dwarfs who lived underground, of men transformed into flying animals, and of eerie howling noises that came from everywhere and nowhere.

Noises at the cave were rampant. No doubt, these sounds were merely from the violent winds that whipped mercilessly through the jungle trees mixed with gusts of hot ocean air that crooned high among the miniature stalactites and stalagmites within the cave.

These were sorrowful tunes. Lamentations, like a grief-stricken mother weeping for her lost child.

As hunger is the best cook, so too are adventure and tragedy the best ingredients for a storyteller. This hard-to-believe tale of Suluan begins here within this very cave, on these remote cliffs, situated above the crystal-blue Pacific waters in Southeast Asia.

This is not a make-believe tribal legend or an old wives' tale passed down over the years. This chronicle is true.

The cave somehow seemed strangely out of place so high up in the air. It looked like an ancient arthritic growth on the north eastern side of the island, as if the cave rose out of nowhere. It bordered a tangle of lush trees and sprawling tropical bush. The cave was a cool retreat from the heat of the sun-sweltering Asian-Pacific weather.

Gaping jaws encircled the entrance. Protruding teeth of rugged rocks in all shapes and sizes created a haunted door of welcome; the cave beckoned its guests to enter.

Someone of great wisdom had built this cave with the foreknowledge that someday it would serve as a place of commencement. Or so it seemed.

Much more than a natural occurrence of nature or evolution, it stood as a providential tower-like landmark on the island.

Facing the great sea, the gargantuan shark's mouth of an entry sucked in the wild and unpredictable forces of nature and then calmed them. Looks can deceive, however. As looming and large-mouthed as the cave's entrance appeared from the outside, people said it felt friendly and small once inside. The cave had a life-saving purpose high on the mountainside.

Because unexpected storms around Suluan occurred as often as most barangays in the Philippines hosted a fiesta, the monstrous canopy was a welcome emergency refuge offering protection from the capricious typhoon weather, against wicked winds and pelting downpour.

Rather than a place to avoid and fear, the cave was now loved. Weather-beaten and old, and though still surrounded with mystery, it had become a place of safety and salvation.

Inside, the craggy damp walls and arched, uneven ceiling were composed of lightly-colored rock, which provided a sturdy castle-like feel to the place. It smelled salty and somewhat stale, and the interior looked like the hull of an ancient capsized ship washed ashore and left to rot with dry seaweed and sour, sun-bleached seashells. Numerous shards of small muscles, crushed pieces of pale coral, shiny rocks and broken pastel shells carpeted the floor of this pale gray grotto.

How the shells got up so high was a mystery. There they were, a wall-to-wall quarry for the treasure-seeker, strewn in and around shallow puddles of murky water. The mini ocean floor covered the huge cavern and provided a soft padded cushion for its bare-footed guests. With every step came the echo of a comfortably solid crunch.

This particular cave, secure like a mother's womb, served as a launching point into an unforgettable voyage. For fifteen brave island friends and their infantile hopes, the cave stood as a symbol of home. Similar to a sacred gravesite, it still stands strong, reminiscent of a consecrated burial place for holy dreams.

Held safe within its craggy walls were the whispered secrets of its guests: unfulfilled years and abandoned aspirations of youth soon to be etched into the history of Suluan, recorded memories kept alongside those of early

Spanish explorers and foreign missionaries. All memoirs of good intentions, things meant to be, eternal epitaphs to optimism.

Like a holy shrine, this cave became a place known on the island where vibrant youth met tragedy, where life washed ashore and returned to begin anew.

Only the bold, or a foolish teen, would march on hot days through the muggy jungle and up to the cave. One had to hike through a complex path that wound through, under, over, and between standing and fallen trunks of giant palms and untamed bush. This vegetation covered the width and breadth of the island and created an airtight canopy above, enclosing stifling humid air beneath.

From a heavenly perspective, the form of the island was much like an odd-shaped salad bowl filled with jade florets of broccoli. Seldom did anyone venture through the wilderness up to the cave by the cliff.

Due to its ill-omened status, it was quite rare that curious teens, or adults, for that matter, undertook the laborious hike up to the cave. However, times had changed. The new generation of youth on Suluan was brave.

On this day in May 1937, the cool cave provided a place of solitude and asylum for two Filipina girls. Earlier, as the sun rose, the two friends had climbed up the side of the mountain. They didn't have permission to do so, exactly, but no one said they couldn't.

The sun filtered through the long and lanky palm leaves attached to statuesque trees far above their heads. These lofty, leafy crowns looked much akin to old-fashioned ceiling fans attached to long poles that freely swayed. They offered little help to stir up a breeze or alleviate the intense tropical heat.

Heavy, moist air clung like a wool blanket to their skin. If the air around them had been water, the teens would have drowned in its steamy thickness. It was difficult to breathe in this heat. Today's escape was the cave, a place of shade and coolness.

Their school vacation allowed Antonia and Bevs time to roam through the jungle. Every day this week the girls wandered up the mountainside together. Stepping over prostrate vines and low-growing shrubs, they held on to each other and trudged on like soldiers.

The narrow path, beaten down by their barefooted hikes, led them to their destination atop the cliffs. These girls had been born on Suluan. It was home, and it was all they knew.

In their eyes, the cave was no longer mystical or forbidden. Rather, the spot had become the harbor for their own private world. The cave became a hidden shelter from the adult world in the village below, welcoming the two best friends to come in and float on their teenage dreams. The rough-hewn sanctuary of cool stone enclosed them in safety.

Unbeknownst to their hovering parents, the girls journeyed to the cliff's edge frequently. Out beyond the door of the cave, shadowy images floated along the ocean's vast horizon: obscure, foreign, and unattainable. These unreachable islands were of no interest to the teens today.

School was out, and their daily chores at home waited. Older people down in the fishing village took advantage of mid-morning siestas to escape the sweltering heat. The rainy season was coming; the humidity was so high it stifled activity.

Movement was slow. Grandmothers sat on old rattan stools in the shade with stacks of tattered clothes to mend on their laps. Grandfathers, with familiar stories and jokes to tell, sat content with their friends looking out to sea and beyond.

Most fathers were out to sea, fishing. Some men, who had been fishing all night, were home cleaning their gear and repairing their nets. Young mothers, wearied after laboring over mountains of hand-washed laundry, gathered in groups to chatter in the shade under peacefully swaying palm trees.

In earshot of these families at rest, boisterous naked children frolicked in the clear shallows of low tide. Cool, sparkling waves splashed over them on their salty playground. Children escaped the lethargy of mid-day that slowed the adults to a standstill.

Peals of their laughter filled the hot summer air. The sliver of an ivory-speckled beach spilled out into the sea and became a wide creamy floor beneath their splashing chocolate feet.

Worn-out fishing boats, with and without outriggers, swayed at the water's edge. Tethered canoes faded from the sun rocked side by side on the shoreline like old friends. Each was tied taunt, lest a sudden stormy gale arrive unannounced to whisk the fishermen's only source of income out to sea. Fishing boats with their long wooden paddles were valuable, like children and houses.

Today, the customary whipping wind from the ocean was at rest. No howling or screeching within the cave. All was still.

Outside of the cave, however, jungle birds cajoled and squawked. Their antics intensified as Antonia stood to her feet, stretched, and meandered out from within the cave to the rim of the rocky cliff.

She stood five feet tall with dark, almost black Asian eyes and a flat nose. Her long hair was black like coal and thick like the forest. It hung down heavy and straight, almost touching her waist.

Her body hovered gracefully on the last precipice of childhood. She carried herself like a dancer; she stood not slump-shouldered, but held up in the small of her back and in the graceful lift of her strong neck.

She had lived only a decade and five brief years and had encountered few things in life that troubled her. Antonia's mama, Macaria, was a very religious woman who led the small Catholic women's group on Suluan called *"the Antoniana"*. Antonia knew that was where she got her name.

Home was peaceful, except when her father was gone too long at sea. Worry then came in waves and spilled into every dusty corner of their lives. This had been part of the fiber of the Arceno family for as long as she could remember. She and her older siblings had learned to live with her mother's frequent tears.

Not all fishermen's wives were so concerned when their husbands failed to return. This constant fear from her mother often infected Antonia. But Bonifacio, her father, always returned safely from the sea. His large, muscular body was strong and healthy from years of hard work – fishing and farming. Bonifacio was a survivor, but Macaria was a worry-wart.

Antonia was one of the smartest girls in her high school, and she was patient and hard-working. Like a magnet, Antonia drew friends to her effortlessly. Her school was located not on Suluan but Guiuan, a larger town that was a three-and-a-half-hour paddle-boat ride west of Suluan on the eastern side of the island of Samar. During the school year, she attended class there and came home every other month.

When she was away, her mother never worried. She knew where her girl was: on solid ground, in good company, safe and secure.

Antonia stretched her limbs wide and hugged the panoramic seascape before her.

"Oh... my..." Antonia said as she spread her rich brown arms out long, side to side. They glistened with coconut oil in the sun. "I love it up here!" The horizon of blue sky melted into blue water, blurring into a watery, hazy vision of a seamless world. "Maupay! How beautiful is this day," she whispered slowly in her Wary-Wary dialect. "Another ordinary miracle of a day. I'm glad to be alive."

Wide eyes surveyed the expansive ocean before her, and Antonia sighed.

"I feel like I could drown in blue. This world is an infinite palace of blue where sky kisses earth!"

She picked up a handful of stones, tossed them one by one down over the cliff, and listened to them hit the rocks below. Plop. Plop. Plop.

"There definitely is a God. He is definitely big! And He really must love blue, don't you think, Bevs? It must be one of His favorite colors."

With a broad smile, Antonia peeked over her shoulder to view her life-long companion. Beverly squatted inside the cave, impatiently trying to untangle her knotted hair with a broken tortoise shell comb.

Bevs made no comment.

Antonia spoke louder; she wanted her friend to dream along with her. "Oh, Bevs, how small we are in comparison to the great sea! I guess we could never be lost; He knows where we are. No sea is too deep for Him, is it? Nowhere is too far. No current is too strong."

She flung another handful of stones carelessly over the edge.

"We must be like a speck of sand... or smaller yet, like a piece of dust. Sometimes, when I stare out on the waves and sky, I feel so alone... so lost and insignificant, don't you?" Silence. "At least we have each other."

Bevs wasn't listening.

Frustrated, Bevs had given up on her knotted hair. She spread out a woven mat and arranged the picnic lunch she and Antonia had carried up the mountainside. Bevs was always busy and distracted with one thing or another.

Beverly had grown up alongside Antonia on Suluan. Their parents, grandparents, and great-grandparents had all been close friends. More than likely, the girls were related in some remote way. And so it made sense that Bevs was part of the Arceno family.

The two girls were as close as sisters could be. However, Bevs was different from Tonya. Her highly organized, serious outlook on life was a direct contrast to that of her taller, thinner friend. Bevs had a critical eye -- a more somber view of life, not quite as idyllic as Antonia's. Bevs collected shells and beautiful rocks; she didn't toss them over cliffs. She loved to cook, while the sanguine Antonia would rather sing before and during a meal than prepare it.

Bevs was immaculate and structured in all she did; Antonia was scattered, spontaneous and carefree. Antonia's eyes were wide and childlike; Bevs saw her world through eyes that were thinly slit, cautious, and wise.

"What a sad thought... to be without you. Have you ever wondered what it would be like if you one day didn't have any friends? What if we had to leave our home, or our parents, or if pirates kidnapped us or if a whale swallowed us while we swam? *Bevs*?"

Bevs ignored her friend's chatter.

"Oh, never mind...."

Antonia returned to her ocean of dreams and to contemplations of the measureless sea below. Her thoughts drifted lazily to philosophical musings of her small, uneventful life on Suluan. *I wonder what would have happened if the King of Spain had never sent out Magellan to discover our country? Suluan would have never been found. What if Magellan had turned back and given up? Or worse, what if he and his companions had all died at sea?* Antonia shuddered with the thought.

The enormity of the expansive waters left her awe-struck, as it did every time she stood on this spot. She scanned the horizon from north to south and back again. She squint her eyes against the harsh sunlight.

Maybe there is something to exploration. Hmmm. I wonder. "You never know what's out there unless you go looking. Di ba? Don't you agree, Bevs? *Bevs?*"

"I don't like sailing. I can't swim. I am afraid of the currents around Suluan. And I *don't* think riding around on a ship for months on end would be very interesting. And...I can't find the papaya salad I know I packed this morning," said Bevs from inside the cave.

Antonia made no comment. She hadn't really listened, either. Her eyes danced over the horizon once again as she surveyed the waters.

Suluan was the farthest eastern Philippine island in the Pacific Ocean. To the far north, China; to the south, she knew there were hundreds, maybe thousands of other islands. To the southwest were islands she had only heard about from her father, her uncles, and the fishermen fathers of her friends.

However, she had never visited these islands herself. She didn't really want to, and had never even considered it, not until today. Out east beyond Suluan's simple shoreline was nothing but endless water -- that was all she knew.

"Just the thought of bottomless ocean waters, where I can't touch the sand, gives me the shivers. I can't even imagine how deep and wide the Pacific is; can you, Bevs? How far would we have to go to get to Mindanao, or over to Cebu? Do you have any idea, Bevs?"

No answer came from the cave.

Suluan, "the sea full of currents", held the secrets of a fascinating history. Centuries ago, cruel pirates and brave explorers had traveled by ship through perfidious waters to its shores. Over the years, countless battered ships propelled by the island's fierce tides, had ended up shipwrecked on the rocky beaches of eastern Samar. These stories filled Antonia's imagination, and her mind wandered out to sea and to the pirates of long ago.

"Know what I heard, Bevs? Samar's name comes from "samad", which means wounded or cut. Can you imagine having a name like *that*! 'The injured island.' How would *you* like to be an island where boats crashed onto *your* shores? No wonder it has such a dreadful name. It's such a rough and rugged place! Ay! How would *you* like to crash into land? Pretty tragic, I'd say."

Bevs moaned. "Oy, Tonya, come on, *please* stop talking such nonsense."

Over the years, Antonia's Suluan had remained isolated and primitive. The islands nearby were encircled by the Pacific Ocean, the Philippine Sea, Celebes Sea, Sulu Sea, and South China Sea, and these waters separated Suluan from the range of all these other islands.

Antonia lived at the end of the earth. At least, that was what she thought the first time she saw a map of the Philippines and had trouble locating where she lived. The map of multiple islands of many queer shapes and sizes looked to her like a puzzle torn apart with its pieces scattered on a table of blue. She looked for her piece of the puzzle: modest little Suluan.

Over 7,000 islands in the Philippine archipelago, and Suluan was the farthest speck of an island in the eastern waters. It rested along the Pacific Ring of Fire. Most people did not even know it existed.

Disconnected. Drifting. Detached. A few modern conveniences had trickled in to Suluan, but it still had no electricity, paved streets, stores, or public transportation. Suluan was one and a half miles long, not very wide, and barely developed.

Homes roofed with rusty metal, grass, or nipa thatch made up the compact center of town. Earthen paths trodden firm over the years separated the simple dwellings. Only a few small houses stood apart from the others, built farther in under the trees.

Suluan had an abundance of banana trees, coconut trees, root crops, fishermen, and fishermen's wives, but there were not rice fields. Imported rice came to them only every other month from the larger island of Samar to the west.

Eastern Samar, the island where Antonia attended high school, was much larger than Suluan. Because of its size, it was connected to the rest of the country. Through Samar, Antonia had heard that one could reach harbors with large ships in cities with interesting names like Tacloban and Ormoc.

Farther west was the island of Leyte, and even farther west the long, banana-shaped island of Cebu. However, her island world here was compact and uncomplicated. Westerners would think her world was both native and naive.

In the transparent waters directly below the cliff, Antonia spotted a school of fish swimming aimlessly under rippled water. The fish were simple, like Suluan. They had no worries, no need for technology and new inventions. They swam unhindered and free just below the surface.

An invisible bond held these colorful fish together;

they flowed unopposed as one, despite wind, waves, or currents. Their simplicity spoke to the heart of Antonia each time she watched them.

Salty sea air filled her nostrils. The rich aroma of the earthy jungle vegetation rose and intensified in the heat of late morning. Antonia's long black hair was still damp and clung to her neck after the long climb up the mountainside. Her slightly tattered skirt stuck to her sweaty legs. Her pale pink floral blouse was tucked neatly into her waistband.

Oh, to jump down into the cool blue waters and swim with the dolphins! To be like a fish would be wonderful! To ride the waves would be freeing.

Octopus, squid, and bright blue starfish gathered underwater, far away from where she stood. The ground beneath her bare browned toes was solid and secure; it held her fast to her island world. Locating distant islands right now was a wearisome task. She would much rather concentrate on things closer to home. Antonia was lost in her fantasy.

She softly blew the ocean a kiss, gracefully placing her hand on her lips and flinging her open hand out towards the surf. Antonia lifted her skirt above her knees, and curtsied before the great expanse. She smiled contentedly.

"Swimming is for fish, I guess not for me."

Antonia belonged in her home on Suluan. Here she was safe and surrounded by love and familiarity. Antonia, like most teenage girls, loved to dream. She admired beautiful things and beautiful imaginings. To dream, however, meant to leave the here and now -- a harmless thing to do as long as these far-fetched fantasies stayed locked up in her mind.

Part of me reaches out — and part of me holds back. Can I dare dream and cling to my home? Can I do both? Does a part of me want to leave? I wish I knew. Like the tangled ropes of dark seaweed in the shallows below the cliff, a chain of contradictions hung around her soul.

Antonia was about to begin her second year of high school after break. School had become quite important to her as well as to her parents. She was no longer a child who ran carefree at the water's edge from dawn to dusk.

True, she and Bevs often still played along the seashore, untroubled and barefoot like children. However, inside she knew that she had already entered into a new chapter of life. Simplicity somehow was slipping away. The thought made her sad.

Confusion had begun to enter her world. She felt forced to let go of the innocence and charm of childhood. Harder still was accepting these staggering new thoughts of growing up – of responsibility – and perhaps someday to leave her home and family.

No. I never want to leave. I don't want to drift out into the unknown. Not even a whisper of a thought challenged her.

Ease and uncomplicated routines had etched their mark in her down-to-earth soul. Suluan provided comfort and shelter from the storms of the modern world – she was hidden and remote. Just like the cave made her feel that morning.

CHAPTER TWO
THE FRIENDS

Bevs put the last huge palm leaf down under the slices of pineapple. She neatly arranged the split coconut shells on the floor of the cave. In her meticulous way, Bevs had every detail of the meal well planned and organized. She had carefully filled the coconut shells with freshly prepared seaweed salad and mounds of dried fish. Then all of a sudden, a loud whoop and holler came out from under the trees.

Surprised, Antonia stepped back from the grassy overhang and her world of dreams.

"Who in the world is up here? Bevs, I think we have company!" Both of the girls began to laugh.

A rowdy gang of their friends suddenly appeared and tromped toward Antonia. They marched single file on a thin path through the last few feet of forest and then spilled into the open space, practically tumbling out on top of each other. Sweat-soaked from head to toe, they were young men full of life and drenched with boundless energy.

Nine boisterous teenage boys toppled into the girls' private world, descending upon them like an unexpected storm. Their raucous playfulness had increased over the past few years; jokes, tricks, and physical tests of strength from these princes of the island had become the norm.

Today would be no exception.

Antonia flashed a welcome smile. "Hey! What a surprise *this* is!"

She looked over each boy, one by one, and scrutinized each form, each muscle, and each appearance of emerging manhood. These, the good-natured boys of her small village, were family to her, like her own older four siblings at home.

There, she was the baby of the Arceno family. However, here with these boys, she was Antonia, the young woman. Antonia, a girl grown up, stood among young men who found her attractive and fun. Her heart raced at their unexpected arrival.

Carlo led the group, since at age nineteen he was the oldest. He planned to marry Daisy at the end of the week. Antonia assumed Daisy and the rest of the girls were still climbing up the mountainside. Carlo and Daisy were the first from this band of companions to pair up.

In true Filipino fashion, they sought permission from their parents first to court and then to wed. This practice had come to the country through the Spaniards hundreds of years ago.

Carlo was tall, strong, and lanky. His deeply tanned face bore slight scars and pock marks here and there. Nothing, however, could mar his handsome features and engaging disposition. He wore a sincere smile and was a natural leader of the boys. Carlo's grandparents had raised him.

His grandpa, known to everyone as Papa Beni, was a fisherman as well as a farmer. Papa Beni's sweet countenance and gentle manner were his trademarks. Beni's two front teeth slightly overlapped and protruded a bit. They stood out because on either side all other teeth were missing, giving him a rabbit-faced grin.

Honed from years of hard work, Beni's rugged hands

and tightly-packed muscles made him appear much younger than he was. Papa Beni had a strappingly strong physique and a humbly quiet personality. For decades, he had grown old and tended to his small coconut and banana plantation. Like the other men on Suluan, he spent much time fishing at sea.

Carlo's grandma, Mam Salud, was like a second mother to Antonia. While Beni was short and compact, Mam Salud was large-framed and a bit plump. To fall into her big arms in a warm embrace was to sink into a cushion of love. She enjoyed cooking and eating as well. Salud now served her fourth term as barangay captain of Suluan. She governed the entire island with persuasive, charismatic charm. This was especially helpful when she made decisions and researched prospects to bring small improvements onto the island.

Some concluded that she bought votes year after year through bribery, but this was not so. Salud was one of the few honest politicians in her day. She was the perfect woman for the job, since it was her nature to be sincere and strong.

Political savvy and family connections on the big island of Luzon had helped her supply the cement to build steps to the lighthouse near the cave. Numerous relatives spread out like a net on many islands provided favors and assistance for Suluan. With their help, Salud slowly made improvements to the living conditions all over the island.

Salud was a mover and a shaker in her own right; she was smart. The workforce to build the steps was under her command. She alone drew up the design, and she oversaw the entire building process.

Carlo had lost his parents in a freak fire when he was eight. Nightmarish memories of his house bursting into flames still clung to his soul. Apart from his deformed right ear and the scarred markings on his nose and cheeks, Carlo's demeanor was seemingly unscathed. He was healthy, stable, and tough.

But the under-the-surface emotional world of Carlo was sorely blemished with the pain of loss. His confident personality was a product of the steadfast love and careful guidance of his dear grandparents, and at times it served as a decoy to avert attention from his true struggles.

Carlo? Soon to be a married man?, mused Antonia.

Antonia looked down at her feet, dug in her toe, and pushed around a pile of small shells. She felt sadness rise within her.

He can't be leaving Suluan.

She still could not grasp this slow-moving reality; her heart had not caught up with the truth in her head. Into her constant, never-changing view of life on Suluan, the picture of Carlo getting married did not fit well. Daisy, whom he had met when he attended school in Guiuan, was the lucky girl who had stolen his well-protected heart.

Antonia sat still.

He found something -- someone there in the town of Guiuan not found on our island. Daisy is an import.

Antonia struggled to accept this fact. Their wedding was just a couple of days away. Ate Daisy will be a beautiful young bride, and kuya Carlo a fine-looking groom.

Antonia shook her head in disbelief. She thought back to the time when she and Carlo had played as little children. They had spent hours together sitting on the bamboo-slatted floor of her home. He had always been a big brother to her and now, all grown, he was a calm voice in her life.

She remembered his kindness and affection of fifteen years. Antonia had done her best in the last several years to attract and amuse him. Despite her charms, Carlo had found Daisy. How was she to bear his leaving?

Carlo caught her off guard with a playful wink.

"Hey, Day," he said. Day, pronounced "di," and meant little sister. "We men came up to keep you girls safe from the Wok-Wok! You know, don't you, Tonya... I'll be getting married, and this might well be the last time we have together at the cave. Mam Salud cooked all this for us."

He motioned to the heavy-laden baskets of food the boys lugged on their shoulders.

"The girls are close behind us with all your favorite dishes. I'm ready to have my own pre-wedding fiesta, kinda' like my last supper with my best friends!"

Carlo was exuberant as he dropped his load of food and swept Antonia up off her feet. He twirled her around until they were both dizzy and out of breath.

"Day... you *are* happy for me, aren't you?" he whispered in her ear as he carefully set her down.

Surprised by this unexpected question, she blushed and covered her mouth with her hand. Lowering her eyes, she tried to hide her embarrassment. Her heart skipped a beat as she thought of herself cradled in his arms. How she would miss his playfulness.

"Manong Carlo, how could you ever think that I am not the happiest person for you on this entire island? I'm counting the minutes until we take you and manang Daisy to Guiuan to see you two walk down the aisle! Uh... I think I was shocked to see you... and everybody, for that matter... up here.... That's all."

Carlo's best friend, Amado, came from behind at that moment. He wrapped his thick arms tight around Carlo's shoulders and shook him from side to side.

Amado slapped him hard on the back and said jokingly, "Yeah, my 'barcarda' since forever. My best friend is leaving me for a girl! I forgive you, bai, good friend. An island girl has snagged you. Ay! It can happen to the best of us! So long as we can still meet now and then to fish and play cards, I will let it go this time."

Amado laughed his hearty belly laugh. He loved to laugh at his own jokes. Through wide, soft eyes he smiled at Antonia and gave her a knowing look. They would all miss Carlo.

Amusing Amado was a broad-shouldered, round-faced seventeen-year-old with a loud mouth. His boasting was mostly in jest and never mean-spirited or cruel. He flaunted his abilities, which were many.

He was the best singer in eastern Samar. Awarded first place at most fiestas, he had competed in vocal contests since he was a small child. Therefore, people expected him to seek a career in films and to move to Manila, where one of his uncles lived. Give Amado a crowd and a guitar, and he could entertain his fans for hours on end.

"I can bring a dead man to tears with my love songs," Amado used to say. He and Antonia often sang duets together, as she also had a beautiful voice. Amado had a heart for children. He had no desire to assume the role of a fisherman, like his father. Nor did he long for the big city life of Manila.

His dream was to finish school and then do the unthinkable: attend college. After that, he wanted to settle down as an elementary teacher where the pay was good and then, hopefully, father a large brood of children all his own.

Antonia enjoyed Amado's personality. As the village joker, Amado saw to it that he was always in the center of the action. He had a knack for making everything fun and unpredictable. Antonia was one of his greatest fans.

Several of the boys saw Bev's set-up of the girls' picnic lunch at the mouth of the cave and descended on her like a team of fine waiters. They came with baskets, covered wooden bowls, and blackened aluminum pots of warm food.

Exuberant young men pulled out dozens of woven bags, the size of a child's fist, of hanging rice. Then piles of sweet, juicy mangoes appeared. At last, the boys placed a pot in the center of the feast. It was hot caldereta stew, made from Papa Beni's slaughtered goat.

There were huge bunches of bananas, fried tuna fish, kinilaw (raw fish soaked in vinegar and spices), sticky rice delicately rolled up in banana leaves and soaked in coconut milk and brown sugar, barbeque chicken, and several pitchers filled with buko, refreshing baby coconut juice.

After a minute, the meager spread intended for the girls' lunch had transformed into a veritable native feast. The aroma of many spices filled the air within the cave. Bevs was thrilled with all these unexpected visitors and delicacies, and she stood to thank the boys with her sweet smile.

"I *love* all this!" she said. "Salamat! Thank you, boys."

The rest of the boys unloaded more neatly-wrapped packs of food, and Bevs began organizing each new fragrant arrival.

All at once, a group of four weary girls emerged from under the low-hanging branches. They had struggled to climb up the last steep leg of the overgrown mountain trail.

Their faces glowed when they saw Antonia and Bevs' surprise. They pushed back their tousled hair and wiped the moisture from their brows. Each girl straightened her rumpled blouse.

Trademark Filipina smiles in place, they embraced Antonia and Bevs with the tenderness and warmth of old friends. Hand in hand, they all took a good look inside the cave, where the party was about to begin.

The group was complete. This would be a despidita: a farewell, good-luck, we-love-each-other celebration in advance of the wedding. Antonia stared at her Suluanon friends. She wanted to permanently record this picture in her heart as one of the happiest moments of her life.

Oh, if only we could all remain here on Suluan -- young, free, and simple.

Surely they were meant to stay together always, linked like the school of fish, hidden among seaweed and untouched by storms.

She stepped back from the group chatter for a moment to wipe her eyes. A feeling of unexplainable sadness came over her. Antonia struggled without saying a word or allowing her expression to betray her. She would rather not share her doubts with the happy group.

Antonia looked out over dazzling sparkles of blue sea. She strained her eyes looking for a reassuring sign along the endless horizon or within the infinite heavens above that all would be well. Antonia felt restless and uneasy; she could not shake the queer feeling that something was not right.

Her eye caught sight of a dark cloud that loomed far off. It was only the size of a small coconut, but nonetheless, she took this as an omen. Filipino superstition banged on the door of her heart. This wicked trespasser, this uninvited guest, challenged her carefree party.

Lita, her rather bossy cousin, yanked at Antonia's elbow and pulled her back into the circle of friends. She gave Antonia a stern look of disapproval and a quick pinch at her waist.

Lita was a stocky girl with a somewhat boyish demeanor. She had a crooked, grimace-like smile with some teeth missing and others turned partially black. Lita's furrowed forehead set off by her heavy eyebrows silently conveyed her demands. She was the only one in the group who seemed annoyed with Antonia at times.

Offering Lita a weak nod of obedience and respect, Antonia rejoined the group, turning her back to the ocean and its voice. Antonia shut her eyes and tried to quiet her anxious thoughts.

No way; I cannot allow anything to spoil these last few days before the wedding. For Daisy, for Carlo, for Papa Beni and Nana Salud, this must be the most memorable week of our lives!

She returned to her smile and took her place on the gray-shelled floor of the great cave. Wedged in shoulder to warm brown shoulder, Antonia sat between Bevs and Lita.

Without a word, they reached automatically for one another's hands and bowed their heads. Peter, the shy and quiet son of a widower fisherman, began a simple prayer of praise and thanks.

"For friends," he prayed, half-singing, "for adventures, for new life, for what lies ahead and what we will never forget. Thank you for Suluan."

"Yes, amen," said Antonia in a soft voice. "Thank you, Lord God, for destiny!"

Heads stayed bowed, and a holy hush rested on the group. Something reverent filled their cavern-turned-dining room. No one dared move, nor speak. Carlo slowly raised his half-filled cup of coconut juice. He whispered a toast to his best friends.

"To forever friends, for all eternity, together through thick and thin... nothing can separate us."

Antonia dared to lift her head to peek at Carlo. Her heart raced, and her mouth went dry.

Carlo is leaving. We're being ripped apart.

His voice cracked with emotion. They all broke out in gales of laughter, mostly to cover up their embarrassment. The placid cave walls echoed the mirth of the moment.

Amado opened the lid on a pot of rice and looked around sheepishly.

"Ako gutom! I'm hungry!; let's eat!" he yelled.

Typical Amado, always hungry.

They ate all together with talk and laughter, with storytelling and gossip, with fingers dipped from pot to mouth and back. Good food connected Filipino hearts and satisfied their love of family.

After they could eat not one more kernel of sticky rice, the full-stomached boys stood up and moved about slowly with long, satisfied sighs, unabashed burping, and groans of contentment.

The young men walked to the edge of the cliff to stare out to sea. They stood silently, side by side, with arms flung over one another's shoulders or linked together around a waist.

They fit together like an old picket fence. Some of its posts were tall and thin, while others were short and stout; some bent forward, while others pulled back. But the fence had grown strong over the years; in spite of their differences, they all belonged.

The waves crashed angrily on the rocks below, a reminder that the great waters of the Pacific could be merciless when they chose. The wind had picked up, and so had the movement of the sea. It teetered on the brink of a bad mood; the sea seemed ill at ease.

Sons of fishermen, well-schooled from their fathers, these teens knew the rough, complex waters of the Pacific as well as they knew one another -- or so they thought. Today, however, their attention was elsewhere.

CHAPTER THREE
THE LIGHTHOUSE

Raucous whoops and hollers broke the silence of the boys' belly-full hush. Jhun, Ofelia's oldest brother, challenged the others to a race up to the lighthouse that loomed high above the cave. It was a monument both in height and history.

The name Suluan, meant "the place where the lighthouse is" or "torch-bearing people," in reference to the local fishermen who used torches to fish at night. Farther on up into the thicket above the cave, 490 concrete steps led to the whitewashed cement lighthouse.

The boys took off toward the sloping lighthouse steps, bounding higher, higher, fighting and elbowing one another to see who could outrun the others to the top. The boys were physically fit and strong, but the heat and the steepness of the slope challenged even the strongest of men.

Momentary exhaustion gripped all of the boys halfway up. Once they caught their breath and wiped their sweaty faces, off they went again. The young men pushed and shoved their way to the summit. Their legs felt like rubber, and their lungs wanted to burst as they gasped for air.

"Don't give up, men!" yelled Carlo over his shoulder.

He thought of Daisy sitting below with the girls in

the cool cave, and just the thought of her spurred him on to keep going.

Domingo, nicknamed Doming, groaned in a raspy voice, "We're all *crazy!*"

The boys ignored the temptation to rest. This was the psychological trick they used to climb up the steps. They pumped their legs, faster, faster, to climb one cement step after the other. No boy acknowledged the cramps in his legs; no one ever admitted weakness. They kept their eyes ahead, resisting the enemy of pain and defeat.

"You can do it -- you're *all* heroes!" Carlo chanted as he neared the top.

Rey, the shortest and fastest of the teens, was the first to arrive. He stood at the top, panting and out of breath but with his roguish smile still in place. He had removed his t-shirt on the way up and draped it over his head to protect himself from the blazing afternoon sun. His black eyes twinkled; his longish dark hair, now soaked with sweat, framed his small, round face. His banter and repartee of tricks were in full swing today.

From under the shade of his dangling, dampened shirt, he cheered each one over the finish line. Rey even had a word of encouragement for Roger, who, due to his size, lumbered up the final section of steps last of all. Roger's wide chest heaved. He fell panting into the arms of his friends like a dead man.

"Oh God... I can't go on," he said.

Roger was big for his age. Though he was a bit clumsy and slow, he always protected the girls. His bangs hung low over his eyes, and he had a tendency to hide behind both his hair and his friends.

At fifteen, he was quieter and more pensive than the other boys. Roger was not the brightest in his studies, but what he lacked in brains, he made up for in willingness to help others.

Once all the boys caught their breath on the landing, they perched like birds round about on the rocky retaining wall. Inspired by this lofty look-out point far above the cave and the ocean below, they began an animated discussion about the exploration of ancient seamen.

Mario, the adventure seeker of the group, recited the story of Ferdinand Magellan, the Portuguese-turned-Spanish explorer who had discovered the Philippines in 1521.

"You know, they were brave explorers who first discovered our island," he began.

Carlo, Amado, and Rey sprang to their feet, ripped long banana leaves off a near-by tree, and fashioned pirate-looking headbands around their heads. Doming and Alfredo, two brothers, took bolo knives out from underneath their belts and began a comically staged sword fight. Mario continued with his history lesson.

"As I was saying," he paused and raised his voice louder. "Magellan was a great sailor who sailed on behalf of the King of Spain, but he was originally from Portugal." His voice trailed off as the bolo knives clashed in front of him.

The two siblings fought every ten minutes or so. They found opportunity to wrestle, punch, slap, poke, and jab each other over the slightest provocation. Of course, it was always in fun; they could not imagine life without each other. They had already knocked out a few of each other's teeth, and two years ago Doming accidentally cut half of Alfredo's left thumb off during what they swore was only a playful brawl.

"Come on, let's fight," yelled Alfredo to his brother, interrupting Mario's monologue. "I will chop off your hands now, you brute, you swaggering pirate of the sea!

You can't escape me! We've got true Spanish blood in us — and I'm a hot-blooded fighter!"

That spring, on the other side of the globe, Spain's Battle of Guadalajara raged as the Spaniards struggled in a bloody civil war. Just one month before, German Luftwaffe had bombed Guernica and then flown in their Condor Legion to assist Franco's forces. But the pirate-sailor boys on this island were unaware of war in Spain.

Here on Suluan, bolo knives swung freely. Roger, Peter, and Jhun took their places before Mario as he continued the story of Magellan's travels for King Charles of Spain. They removed their t-shirts and slung them diagonally across their chests like the European sailors.

They were no longer simple sons of fishermen but mighty conquerors who rode ships across the Seven Seas. The base of the lighthouse became an open stage for the actors to perform their dramatic adventure.

They did not know that years later, this very lighthouse would become the stage for a bona fide battle when American troops, under the command of Captain Arthur D. "Bull" Simons of Company B, would lead a surprise attack to root out hidden Japanese soldiers.

Military history would record that in a daring night attack; part of the company would cut off a security detachment at the foot of the steep trail up to the lighthouse, while other troopers would climb the cliffs, strike the surprised garrison from the rear, and annihilate them. Today the enemy and the battle were only make-believe. The true battle for life was yet to come.

In the background, Mario's voice grew louder and more expressive.

"Daily Magellan's brave Spanish crew," he said with pride, "were dying of hunger and thirst. Their large vessels became wandering cemeteries lost at sea."

His voice trailed off again, and the boys acted out

sailors going insane and dying. They groaned and faltered, slowly stumbling to the ground.

"I am ... dying, washed ashore... insane with fear," cried Rey as he sank to his knees with a thud.

Roger threw his big arms up over his head and let out a blood-curdling scream. "Aaaaaah!" he cried.

Strange, that such a loud sound could come out of such a shy teen. The boys relived these gruesome events like actors on a Broadway stage.

"Right here," Mario's voice rose again with emotion, "here in our very Suluan waters, Magellan discovered the Philippines. Our island was the very first place they dropped anchor. The Spanish armada saw the torches of the fishermen the night before they landed here."

The "dead" sailors rose up off the ground, cheers went up, and the young men saluted and clapped themselves proudly on their bare chests.

"What a story. I wish *I* were a captain of a great ship at sea," admitted Peter.

"Pete, you will be tomorrow, bai, when we sail to Guiuan! I wish *I* had been the one to discover our island," said Carlo. "I would be famous; I'd have a badge for courage."

"Yes, but to get the story right," said Jhun, who was now seventeen and at the top of his third year class in high school, "Magellan only got some food here on Suluan. Then they set sail and continued south to land on Homonhon on March 16th, to be exact, and it was there," he explained, pointing to the far-away island to the southwest of where they stood, "that he dedicated these islands to God and to the King of Spain. Suluan was just a stop-over for him."

Inspired, Mario resumed his storytelling and illustrated in detail Magellan's travels to the central island of Cebu, and of how he was slaughtered with a spear on the small island of Mactan by the tribal chieftain, Lapu-Lapu. Lapu-Lapu was revered from that day on as a hero in the Philippines.

"What a gruesome way to die," said Carlo.

"And…" Mario's voice drifted off, and he spoke in a more reverent tone, "over two hundred brave men died on that voyage. Only a handful ever returned home to Spain. Only eighteen."

"Better eighteen than none," Peter whispered.

"Yeah, sayang, too bad -- those poor guys," Doming responded. "They didn't know the waters like *we* do. The sea won that time."

Carlo stood with his hands on his hips, looking out to the ocean. "Yeah. Sometimes it does."

"Their sailing logs detailed everything, including their discovery of our island," said Mario. "Suluan is now in the history books of the world!" He sighed loudly.

Amado was in his theatrical element. In his whimsical way, he sang an old Spanish love song and paraded around among the boys with his head high, his bare chest expanded and puffed out like a proud rooster crowing. He composed words as he strutted around the lighthouse; Amado crooned of lost love, of bravery, of death, and of the magic of the great sea. His buddies rolled their eyes and groaned.

"Ahhh… you men are too serious for me," Amado taunted at the end of his song.

The boys whooped and shouted so loud even the girls down below heard the noise. Alfredo decided to shimmy up a coconut tree to fetch some coconuts to quench the boys' thirst. He bit into his bolo knife, held it fast between his lips, and with a hop, disappeared over the wall and hacked a new trail through the vegetation.

The trees stood like soldiers around the lighthouse platform, dutiful wooden guards with long, strong arms that stretched around the retaining wall.

Once he located his target, Alfredo scaled about a hundred feet up the smooth trunk of a lanky coconut tree. His skill with the bolo and his agility to balance while cutting down coconuts entertained his friends. He was like an acrobat on a high wire. Chop-chop -- a place for a hand, chop-chop -- a place for the other hand, then one foot, then the other foot.

Another whack with the bolo, and he was higher, carefully moving up and up. Now he cut clean wedges for his hands and bare feet to take hold. Up he continued, rhythmically carving his own ladder into the tree trunk.

"Bet I can do this faster than all of you!"

"Yeah, yeah -- you braggart," retorted his brother below him.

Up under the crown of the palm tree, Alfredo reached into the cluster of lime green baby coconuts and hacked away at them with swift chops from his curved knife. One by one they crashed to the ground below like bombs from a warplane.

By now, his brother Doming stood near the base of the tree, carefully avoiding the falling missiles. He knew that a coconut falling from such heights could kill him if it landed on his head.

"You don't want me dead, do you?" Doming asked.

"At least we won't die of thirst, like Magellan's men," said Alfredo.

"Yeah, yeah... *you're* our hero today. You rescued us all," Doming said.

Alfredo clambered back down to safety. He and Domingo lugged the heavy lime green balls back up to where the boys sat. The brothers sliced off one end of the tough fruit just large enough to open up a small hole from which to drink. Doming handed each of his friends his own coconut and they gulped down the sweet juice enthusiastically.

Amado let the liquid dribble down his chin.

"God knew when He made the Filipino that we'd need a flat nose to drink from the coconut," he said.

Everyone laughed.

After they drank the juice, they cut open the top even wider and used the cut-off piece of coconut as a spoon to scoop out the inside lining of filmy white coconut meat. The paper-thin, translucent gel was always a treat to dig out, no matter how many times the boys had eaten it.

"Sobrang sarap, very delicious," Jhun said.

Peter laughed and raised his eyebrows. "Oy, bai... You speak Tagalog now and not Waray-Waray?"

"Also Spanish, my friend... muy sabroso. It's all the same."

"Here's to our Spanish explorers," Mario said as he lifted his coconut high over his head.

The boys cheered as they raised a native toast. They made their way down the steps and gathered again at the edge of the cliff outside of the cave.

They resumed their brotherly pose along the precipice, locking arms together, hanging on to one another's necks, and leaning against one another's side. They were family.

CHAPTER FOUR
THE WEDDING PLANS

All six girls automatically gathered the leftovers and cleaned up the cave. They picked up discarded fish bones and scattered rice strewn between the rocks where the boys had sat. No one said a word about who did what. No one gave a second thought to why they needed to clean the cave at all. Just like their mothers, the girls adeptly cleaned the cave and all remnants of food out of second nature.

The girls had been trained to model selfless servanthood as the feminine expression of being truly Asian. The Geisha spirit came as easily to young Filipinas as breathing, as naturally as their constant smiles.

After they packed away the few leftovers in fresh banana leaves, they returned the blackened aluminum cooking pots and wooden bowls to the woven carrying baskets nestled in a corner of the cave. Then the girls gathered inside the coolness of the cave to rest and to talk.

They chattered nonstop with talk of the island, of school, and of the wedding, bouncing from one subject to another. The nutty aroma of cooked rice still hung in the air. A cozy, sleepy feeling settled in among the girlfriends.

Antonia sat in the middle of the group. Bevs stretched out and laid her head, with its mass of tangled locks, on her best friend's lap. She was comfortable silently asking for help with her wind-tousled mane. Antonia slowly unraveled the knots and combed Beverly's hair straight and smooth.

Daisy plopped down as close as she could to Antonia. She sought the warmth of friendship that Antonia radiated. Daisy was the only one in the group not born on Suluan, making her somewhat of an outsider. Unlike the other girls, she was not related to anyone in the group.

Antonia made her feel welcome and accepted and hoped the girls would be eager to talk about Daisy's wedding day and the big trip planned for tomorrow morning. But instead their chatter focused mostly on themselves. The hum rose and fell in the cave like the buzz of flying crickets.

The wedding ceremony was all Daisy thought about these days, but she did not want to be the center of attention, so she never brought up the subject. She listened intently to the conversation with a perpetual smile across her face.

On the other side of Antonia sat her dear friend Perla, who, because of her shyness, rarely spoke. Around Antonia, Perla opened up and relaxed. Perla leaned into her and tilted her head casually onto Antonia's shoulder.

Smooth waves of rich black hair tumbled haphazardly below her shoulders. Perla looked at life through timid eyes and greeted it with the most beautiful modest smile Antonia had ever seen.

Perla laid her delicate and perfectly-manicured hand on Bevs' head and began stroking her hair, too. She said nothing but smiled coyly down at Bevs and hummed softly to herself. Perla's thoughts were a million miles away.

Lita, Antonia's bossy cousin, sat cross-legged and

knee-to-knee next to Ofelia. Ofelia was a schoolmate and long-time friend of Antonia. She had a huge birthmark on her cheek, but that never quenched her outgoing nature. Ofelia was the shortest girl in the group and was often teased about her height. She and Lita had been discussing one of the boys' new plans since they arrived. Now the girls were at it again with a new level of intensity.

"Oy!" said Lita rather loudly in her husky voice. "These boys are just boang -- just crazy. They expect us all to leave tomorrow for Guiuan at dawn. I don't think we need to leave so early. Mario told me he wants to fish along the way and make an extra trip to some small island to hunt for crabs."

The girls all shook their heads and clucked their tongues; they wondered how they could possibly squeeze in a crab-hunt. They would still have so much preparation for the wedding to do once they landed on Guiuan.

Ofelia chimed in, "I guess we'll just have to go along and let them have their fun. After all, we need those crabs for the reception. We can go ashore with them to sleep or stay on the boat and work on the decorations. No need to worry, Lit; we've got plenty of time to get everything done."

Lita was not convinced.

She retorted in a somewhat harsh tone, "Ofelia, you just don't have a clue how much work we have."

Everyone knew better. Lita had another reason she wanted to arrive early. Near the end of their school year, she had met a nice young man in Guiuan who flirted with her during their lunch hours. Obviously, she was desperate to see him again.

With a knowing look, Ofelia pressed her lips together and rolled her eyes. She knew that if she said more Lita would be offended, as she often was.

"Yeah, yeah, Lit -- I guess you're right," said Ofelia.

"Of *course*, I know I am!"

Lita's turbulent moods needed support from her friends. It was better to keep quiet than to argue with her. Gruffly, Lita shrugged her shoulders and glanced furtively around the circle with squinted eyes.

The girls cupped their hands over their mouths to stifle their laughter. Lita's face soured even more and turned red. She abruptly swung her head around and ignored them all.

Antonia braided Bevs' hair just as she had done this task a thousand times before. Left over middle, right over middle, left over middle -- the silky black tresses were easy to handle now, untangled, dry, and combed straight. Bevs' braided hair took the shape of the long, tightly woven rope used to tie up sailboats.

The wide braid felt heavy and strong and smelled like coconut oil. Filipinas knew warm coconut oil rubbed into hair would make it shiny, black, and healthy. No one had ever cut any of their hair.

Bevs enjoyed the attention. Smiling out of pure contentment, she sighed and gave in to the tiredness that came after a huge meal. Her eyelids slowly closed.

The cave was cool. The drone of the voices from the boys outside became background music in her head. In no time, Bevs drifted off to sleep. Antonia continued to braid the hair of her now motionless friend.

Eventually, the girls spoke about the upcoming Saturday wedding, much to Daisy's delight. She had listened with patience as they talked about everything except her marriage, just as she had unwearyingly waited for Carlo to propose. She excelled in this business of waiting her turn and hanging on to hope.

Instead of anxiousness, Daisy's personality exuded confidence and inner strength. The waiting produced a deep level of trust in God to guide her paths. Now she saw the fruit of that faith: she was the first among the girls to marry.

The enthusiasm of her love for Carlo was tangible; it filled the very air around her as she spoke of him. Antonia noticed Daisy's beautiful caramel brown skin, set off by a string of small, creamy white seashells hung long around her neck, glistening and shining from the humidity.

She looks so grown up. No wonder Carlo loves her.

Carlo was the man of Daisy's youthful dreams, and she was happy to welcome into her life all these new 'little sisters' from his world on Suluan. They were all younger than her, and perhaps that was why they were a wee bit overly concerned with themselves. Once Antonia opened up the subject of the wedding, the girls dove in and chattered like chickens.

They talked about their dresses, their hair, how they wanted to decorate the church sanctuary, and with what songs they would serenade the newlyweds. Again, Daisy sat quietly and listened. Her smile never faltered.

Antonia skillfully turned the conversation directly to Daisy and asked, "So Ate Dais, where are you and manong Carlo planning on living after you are married? I heard you won't be coming back to Suluan with him, di ba -- is that true?"

Daisy described the small house that they had found to rent in her parents' barrio in Guiuan. Carlo would work with her father in their rice fields along with her uncles and brothers, and Daisy planned to use her skills as a seamstress to start a small business. The young couple figured they would earn enough income to pay for a simple native hut on the edge of town.

Carlo was skillful with his hands, and they had plans to build on to the home as their family grew. In light of the upcoming marriage, Antonia had begun to view

Guiuan as a world away from Suluan and no longer just a neighboring island.

Daisy is so independent. She knows exactly what she wants.

The topics flowed from childbearing, to cooking, to decorating the church, and back to how they would style their hair for the wedding. Antonia studied Daisy, and as she did, she let go of her thoughts of Carlo, like releasing a beautiful starfish back into the sea.

She tried hard to set him free and to grow up. She was happy to see Daisy's cheeks blush and to dream along with her. The marriage to Carlo had every promise of happiness for her new friend.

I'm feeling a bit like water in a storm... but I don't know where my shore is. Why don't I know what direction is mine? I don't even want all these grown-up decisions.

Antonia's chatting friends did not notice her internal anxiety. She hid behind her smile. No one would ever know of her secret love for Carlo or of the pain that now ached deep within her heart. Not even her best friend, Bevs.

The afternoon grew long, and the sun slowly sank around the bend to the right of the cliff, far off in the western sky. Long bands of colorful light came over the lip of the orange-tinted ocean that rippled and shone like a bronzed hot plate. The streaks filled the sky before them, reflecting and bouncing off the water.

Intermittent gusts of blistering hot wind increased ever so slightly, and Antonia from inside the shell of their cave tried to ignore the darkening clouds to the north. The one small cloud she had seen earlier that day had multiplied itself into several.

The boys returned to the cave as the girls gathered their belongings and talked about heading back home. This evening they must pack for the wedding and make final preparations for their three-and-a-half hour sailboat trip to Guiuan the next morning.

Peter, with his neatly cropped curly hair, would be the captain. His father's sailboat was the largest and the only one on the island and could easily hold fifteen youths with all the food, presents, and supplies they planned to bring on their journey. Osting, Peter's father, owned what they called a Kabakaba, – a sailboat with one single enormous sail.

Peter and Mario had made definite plans to stop along the way, as Lita had feared, at a tiny uninhabited island to hunt for an hour or so for crabs for the wedding meal.

"It will do us good to get off the boat and take a break. Besides," Peter said, "we could take a swim together, stretch our legs, and cool off."

At this comment, all the girls' thoughts went immediately to their hair.

"No!" said Lita, "We will not go into the water or into the hot sun. Don't you boys *know* we need to protect our creamy skin and not run the risk of it turning black like… well, like a fisherman's leathery hide?"

"I don't want my hair to turn yellow and dry in the sun," murmured Bevs to the girls, still groggy from her afternoon nap. "I will just stay in the shade and watch."

"Me, too!" said Ofelia and Perla simultaneously.

"Not me," Antonia said, "I know I'm going to jump in and cool off!"

The group wandered to the edge of the cliffs before their long descent down the mountainside. Far out, the water glazed shiny silver on the surface of the sea, interrupted only with wrinkles of orange sunshine.

Jhun threw fifteen small rocks down over the edge; he counted loudly as he threw them, and the friends all watched in silence as the rocks disappeared with a plop into the foamy surf between the boulders far below them.

"Uno, dos, tres, quatro, cinco...." Plunk. Choonk. Pish. Bonk. Each stone made its own unique sound as it entered the water.

Carlo stood behind his Daisy with arms entwined around her slender waist, his chin perched lightly upon her right shoulder. Perla and Ofelia stood close to each other and held hands. Amado and Peter rested their forearms on either side of Rey's squared shoulders. Big Roger squatted on the ground, his hands folded neatly before him between his legs, his head cocked to the side. He, too, was lost again in his thoughts, hidden behind his stringy bangs.

Antonia ventured to break the stillness with a quiet comment.

"Hey, we are so lucky to have each other...."

Everybody just nodded. Though they stood together, each youth was caught up in the thoughts of his or her own private teenage world.

"I don't *ever* want to leave this place. Look how breathtakingly beautiful this view is. There is no other place on earth like Suluan, and this cave, and these cliffs, and our very own lighthouse and the crystal waters at our feet."

"Um, Guiuan is *also* nice," said Daisy, shyly smiling.

Carlo stood up erect and looked around at all his friends.

He nodded and spoke slowly. "Maybe we will someday return to Suluan. Who knows?"

Mario chimed in immediately. "Di pwede! No way! I can't stay put and live like a caged monkey on this dinky island. Look at the sea! It is so open and wide. There is no end to the places we can go! And I don't mean just over to Guiuan."

He was agitated but continued with wonder in his

low, steady voice.

"There is a world to discover out there, and I plan to travel and see every bit! We Filipinos did not win our independence from Spain for nothing. We are free now to come and free to go if we choose!"

"Tinuod. True. *If* we choose," said Antonia. "I don't think I have that explorer spirit in me."

Mario had a personality that hoped for many things. The troubling questions of life had always been part of his everyday conversations. He saw only the vast horizon as he stood on the cliff on this breathtaking day, giving more attention to the sea than to the comments of his friends.

The view unlocked the adventure in his heart and opened to him endless possibilities. However, this worldly outlook inflicted a subtle and uncomfortable challenge on all the rest of the teens, especially Antonia.

Antonia believed in Mario and in his imaginings, and she thought at that moment that he would have made an excellent sailor on Magellan's exploration ships. But his dreams were not hers.

She wished to stay on Suluan forever. She was desperate for the security home gave her. At least, that was what she thought was holding her to Suluan's familiar soil.

Again, a long silence followed.

Perla smiled wryly and whispered loud enough so that everyone could hear, "I think we'd better *choose* to start back. My mother will worry if I'm not home before dark."

Bursts of laughter followed. Bevs nudged Antonia.

"Ah, yes, freedom. Our dear mothers don't give us much of it, do they? I had better hurry back, too. My mom didn't even know I was up here today. Tonya, yours either? They'll think the Wok-Wok got us both!"

Roger sighed loudly. "My mother will think I fell off the cliff."

"Ours, too," said Doming and Alfredo in unison.

With a slight grimace, Antonia whispered, "Mine will think I got lost at sea."

The entrance of the cave on the island of Suluan

CHAPTER FIVE
THE VILLAGE

Ofelia stooped down and helped Perla hoist a heavy sack onto her shoulder. She brushed a few loose strands of wavy hair out of her eyes and turned toward the jungle to go. Everyone followed suit and helped one another down the steep, slippery trail under the trees.

When they could, the girls would walk in pairs, smiling, arms linked gently at the elbow or holding hands; they spoke in whispers punctuated with giggles. The boys joked their way through the brush.

Occasionally they peeled bananas or guava that they picked along their route. Often they stopped to cackle with birds or throw stones at large geckos in the trees.

The fifteen friends shuffled along as soldiers returning from battle, weary from the lighthouse climb as well as from their day of rough-housing in the stifling sun.

The darkness chased them from behind, nipping at their bare heels; the sun set before their faces as they re-entered the village world they knew so well. The sun disappeared in Suluan at six o'clock each day.

By the time they reached the seaside in front of the village, dinnertime fires were ablaze outside every nipa-thatched hut. The smell of cooking rice and frying fish was in the air. Smoke rose from the outdoor "dirty kitchens," making the air hazy and thick.

The boys were hungry again. Children ran back and forth laughing, chasing chickens and barking dogs. They all ran in and around gnarly stumps of trees like athletes maneuvering through an obstacle course.

Each friend said goodnight and departed down his or her own path toward a simple home of either plywood or split bamboo posts.

Large families gathered around tables full of simple, delicious food. Grandparents, parents, children, cousins, aunties, and uncles often ate together and shared what food they had. Hospitality, kindness, and respect for one's elders -- the qualities of home life and domesticity -- were greatly valued and nurtured on Suluan.

Families were vital to the functioning of each community; all of life revolved around the home. The Filipino family was large and extended, yet loyal and closely-knit. People prized the well-being of the family and next of kin above all earthly possessions.

Suluan had no glass, no screen doors, and no fancy architecture. However, the village had a distinct and unique native beauty, the result of its creative and resourceful people who could construct works of art out of the simplest raw materials.

Woven dried palms and parts of the coconut tree formed fanciful shapes to create baskets, fans, and brooms, while split and bent bamboo transformed into distinctive fencing and pieces of furniture. It was native handicraft at its best.

Hanging pots mixed with bright fuchsia and red bougainvillea artistically framed the gabled doorways and pathways to most all of the huts, and the earthen walkways were lined with rusty metal cans filled with sprouting plants of one kind or another.

Delicate gumamela hibiscus flowers flourished abundantly in yellow, white, red, coral or pink colors.

Elegant orchids of every shade, bound with cord to posts and tree trunks, hung everywhere, as if the town were dressed for an upcoming floral fiesta.

Candles and kerosene lamps lit the quickly-approaching night. Close to the water well, a long stone's throw from the center of the town, groups of older fishermen sat in half circles, waiting to be called for dinner. They used stories and humor like bait to entertain one another for hours.

One of the men sat cross-legged on the dirt and strummed his homemade guitar as several around him sang folk songs in deep baritone and tender tenor harmonies with their Waray-Waray dialect. Another group nearby played cards while yet another huddled around a checkerboard and played a game of "dama".

Women scurried about barefoot to pull down their stiffened laundry draped over bushes to dry in the hot sun or hung on fishing line drawn taunt between the trees to flap in the breeze. The many sun-bleached t-shirts that hung on the line were old and ragged, but the women gathered and folded them carefully with motherly love.

Stately palms and wild shrubbery closed in the village at its backside, and protected the residents like a sturdy rear guard. Mother Nature herself sheltered the heart and soul of the island with her greenery.

Thick tropical vegetation grew round about the clusters of homes like an emerald fortress stockade. But Suluan's face lay vulnerable and wide open to the sea.

The water well, or "anoling", was a popular site on Suluan where most of the daytime action took place. Clean, sweet water poured out from under a large rock and gathered in a high-sided square cement pool.

Fresh, non-salty water was here for everyone who came with thirst and a bucket. At anoling, the people washed their clothes and bodies and fetched water to cook and clean at home.

The vast, salty Pacific sea surrounded the small community on all sides. From its continuous briny generosity, these Filipinos made their living.

Suluan wound down on this night with a final flurry of activity: grandparents lit fires, women pulled in laundry, men tied up boats securely onto the shore and cleaned their fishing gear, and children fed their pigs and chickens. Every family member completed chores as routinely as the sun came and went overhead.

Work filled the day from dawn to dusk, whether it was that of chopping vegetables, gutting fish for a meal, carrying water from anoling, hunting for firewood, scrubbing floors with old coconut husks, or washing clothes by hand.

Small fires were blazing at every hut, and the fragrance of roasted pork and fish hung in the air. Since there was no school, children ran and played along the dirt and sand-packed paths without a thought of bedtime.

These joyful urchins took advantage of the extra-long evenings, and it was difficult to corral them into bed so they could close their mischievous almond eyes.

When the little ones finally disappeared for the night, adults gathered by smoldering fires and told stories until late. These were the island cowboys who spun their yarns and passed on legends from the sea.

After she had washed out the pots after dinner, Antonia politely excused herself and meandered from her two-story home into the darkness on the beach only a few yards away. Dark gray water washed the dust off her toes. Soft and cooling, rhythmically slow and steady, it rocked in and out with a clicking, whishing sound over her feet.

She leaned back against her father's faded fishing

boat, and it creaked. He had pulled it half onto shore and tied it snugly to an old stump of a palm tree sticking out of the sand, the way he did every evening when he returned home from his work out at sea.

The heavens above were black-blue. On most nights, a million stars packed the crowed sky. Tonight the sky was a void.

My heart feels like this empty sky. What a night.

Thoughts of Carlo and Daisy consumed her. Antonia's eyes grew wide to take in the vast darkness overhead.

There is no end to these heavens. I wonder what is behind the dark ceiling over me? And what is behind that?

She lifted her face to the black sky. A vast chasm of nothingness stretched out above her as far as she could see. She found no seam where the water stretched out and the sky came down to meet it. Her eyes grew wider. She shut her eyes tightly, and then she relaxed them and tried to focus on the darkness encircling her.

A big gecko in a nearby tree startled Antonia with his piercing "eeh-aah" caw. Extra-large geckos made extra loud noises. His repetitive shrill mating call reminded her of the steady ring of a church bell.

The bells of a Catholic church, she knew, rang at funerals and weddings on the bigger islands. Over and over, in methodical intervals, the lone lizard called out into the darkness.

That's how the church bell will ring at Carlo's wedding on Saturday. Slow and steady. Like a funeral march for me.

Out on the horizon, she saw nothing but a velvety blackness. The infinite black sky met the equally dark water, once again appearing like one seamless world. However, this time it stretched out before her like a huge murky canvas. She shuddered at the thought of no beginning, no end... just eternal darkness.

As she looked off in the distance toward Guiuan where they would travel in the morning, she could barely see the three torch-lit fishing boats anchored about a half-mile off shore in deep waters. Her tears stretched their faint lights into a blur.

She tilted her head back again and closed her eyes to listen to the water as it hit the wooden boat and receded. Tears streamed down her cheeks. Her toes dug into the cool sand, and she wiggled her feet deeper into the muck like crabs wanting to hide.

She thought back over her day: the climb alone with Bevs, their private time together in the monstrous cave, their unexpected guests with food for an army, the dark cloud... then the strange, eerie feeling she had had to fight off in the presence of her best friends, and Carlo's visible love for Daisy.

But then there were the wonderful conversations with her girlfriends and the warm love of friendship she felt for each one of them.

The sun had taken its heat with it to bed, and now a slight chill filled the air. Antonia shivered. She still had work to do tonight. Another call of the gecko interrupted her thoughts. And then her mom's voice rang out and joined that of the gecko.

"Tonya! Tooooonnnnyaaaa...! Come home."

I'd better pack my things and finish the lumpia spring rolls for the wedding.

But she dug her toes deeper into the sand and lingered with thoughts of the wedding.

Antonia had made three hundred of the delicately-filled rolls with her mother, and she needed only to fry them in hot coconut oil on Saturday morning before the ceremony. She and her mom would enfold them in palm leaves this evening by candlelight and bundle them tightly together in an old rice sack. That should see them safely to Guiuan.

Antonia had carefully wrapped her wedding gift a week ago, so it was ready to load onto the boat, too. Earlier in the year, she had hand-woven a set of ten placemats, just as her grandmother had taught her to do when she was a small child.

The intricately woven mats made with baliw, a thick, thorny palm leaf, were interspersed with small shells around their borders. She had first split the leaves lengthwise and then dried them.

After they dried, she had pressed them with smooth wood to soften them before she wove them into a rectangular shape. Antonia had worked on them for months -- day and night and into her summer vacation. They were truly a one-of-a-kind gift.

Antonia's father, Bonifacio, had carved out of beautiful reddish-brown narra wood (the national tree of the Philippines) a set of dishes and serving bowls for the newlyweds, which she planned to bring along on the sailboat tomorrow.

Her whole family's excitement for the big day mounted, and many on the island planned to follow in their own boats early on Saturday morning.

The youth had special permission to travel together on Thursday only because they were such good friends with the bridal pair and needed to go ahead of time to decorate and prepare for the feast.

Daisy's family was expecting hundreds of guests, since they were well known in Guiuan. Such a day of celebration would be quite the event, even in a big town like Guiuan.

Antonia took a deep breath, fixed her gaze somewhere out on the dark horizon and whispered her "*good nights*" to the fish in the deep, to the stars who hid from her view, to the day that had filled her heart, and to her Creator God who was responsible for it all.

She bowed her head and allowed the love from Him she felt within her to rise and overtake every corner of her being. It was challenged by the sadness of losing Carlo. He was leaving her forever. Antonia's heart felt as if it were about to burst.

As she turned to head back to the sleepy village, the gecko sang her away with his chorus.

CHAPTER SIX
THE SAILBOAT

A non-stop background symphony played on the small island, a cacophony of barking dogs and shrill boasts from roosters who crowed without pause or reason. Impolite and enthusiastic roosters served as a nature's own vociferous alarm clock throughout the day.

No one really noticed the racket, as it was a backdrop for life on the island. People on Suluan went to bed early and rose before the sun. However, Suluan never entirely slept.

The sun had set over Suluan. Families were tucked in for the night with the deep gray waters of the Pacific round about them like a blanket. When she finally went to bed, Antonia thought she would not be able to sleep, but it wasn't long before she had dropped off into a deep and unbroken slumber.

It seemed only a few minutes before she felt someone gently shake her awake. She slowly opened her eyes and saw that the room was still somewhat dark, but she could already hear a rustle of activity outside. The old lacy curtains in her sparsely- furnished room gently flapped in and out of the open window, and the day already felt hot.

Antonia reached out for her mother's soft hand and held it close to her cheek.

"Maupay na aga, nanay. Good morning, momma,"

she whispered, so as not to wake the others, who were still asleep. "Salamat. Thanks, ma, for waking me!"

Her mother, Macaria, sat on the wooden frame near her head and tenderly gazed down at her youngest child. Her face was one of fading prettiness, now parted here and there by wrinkles, deep laugh lines, and patches of leathery brown skin. Her expression was one of both tranquility and alertness. As long as her husband, Bonifacio, was not out at sea, she emanated peace.

Antonia took her mother's cool hand in hers and studied it long and hard, turned it over several times, and then pressed it again to her own cheek, which was still warm from sleep. These hands had worked hard over the years and were never idle. Antonia believed with all her young heart that God had blessed her with the most affectionate mother in the world.

How could I ever survive without my mama?

Antonia loved her mother deeply and relished her detailed stories of growing up on Suluan. While they had wrapped up the food together the night before, Macaria had described her own wedding. Antonia, like any curious teenage girl, hung on every word and took the storybook tale of her parents' simple island love and courtship into her dreams that night.

Bevs and Ofelia tapped lightly on the front door of the Arceno home.

"Pssst. Pssst. Maayo! Hello.... Tonya, are you up?" Ofelia whispered loudly.

Antonia slid out of bed, went to her window, and motioned to her friends to come in out of the shadowy darkness to wait while she dressed. Macaria stood up and walked over to her daughter. She gently drew her little-girl-turned-young-woman to her breast and stroked her long silky hair.

Antonia sighed as she listened to the slow and steady

pounding of her mother's heartbeat. She drew strength from her mother's warmth.

Macaria pulled back and cradled her daughter's oval face between her own two hands. She looked deep into Antonia's questioning eyes. Her mother somehow had a sixth sense, as mothers often do, to the state of her daughter's restless heart.

They looked at each other for a long time.

"You will see," started Macaria quietly. "There will be a day for you, too. You are not forgotten, my dearest. Daisy is the right girl for our Carlo. He will be happy in Guiuan, and we'll all see him often. You'll see. Enjoy your sailboat ride today and be my strong girl."

She softly kissed Antonia's forehead and leaned close, the room filled with her motherly gentleness. Her unconditional love reached out as a solace for the unspoken pain of Antonia's disappointment.

"You have an amazing spirit, and I am so proud of who you are. Just turn the pages and write your own story, Tonya. You have so much more to live. Come...you'll see. I know my girl."

Macaria flashed a crooked smile and looked for a response in her daughter's teary eyes. Antonia looked away and wiped her eyes with the back of her hand. A small flicker of encouragement rose up within Antonia as her mom spoke.

She smiled inwardly but did not say a word -- just stared at the floor and swallowed hard. They understood more than either woman had spoken.

I wish I could tell her how I really feel about Carlo. Antonio let out a small sigh. *But I'm really not so sure I know myself.*

"Now get dressed," her mom said, "and go entertain your guests. Your friends are eager to leave, and you don't want to keep them waiting. I've made some hot chocolate and rice porridge for you, and you can take a minute to eat a bit of breakfast with them before you leave for the shore. Okay, na?"

Antonia bit her lip and slowly bobbed her head up and down. Memories of her childhood friend, now about to wed, raced again through her head.

Carlo will soon be out of sight and out of reach.

Macaria picked up her daughter's small travel sack, turned, and padded softly out the door. Antonia slipped into her favorite floral-printed dress and tied her hair back into a smooth ponytail.

She took a long last look around her bedroom before she left to join her friends for breakfast.

Along the water's edge stood a small bevy of onlookers and well-wishers. The nine boys had begun to load the sailboat. They balanced barefoot with their pant legs rolled up to their knees on a one-foot by eight-foot plank that stretched from the shore into the boat, where they handed off baskets and boxes to load into the ship's hull.

Peter and his father stood on board to direct the packing. The two made sure that all cargo balanced, and they tied everything securely in place. The lengthy wooden sailboat rocked slowly back and forth on the small waves that reflected the frail morning sunlight; the mast creaked as it swayed high above all their heads.

A few buckets of fresh drinking water and two dozen live chickens in cages sat among the cargo being loaded for the wedding. The hens cackled together inside a widely-slatted wooden box. Peter's father, Osting, partially covered the boxes with an old rice sack in an attempt to keep the birds calm.

Also among the supplies were a stack of fishing rods, two large nets, four metal buckets for the crabs they hoped to catch, and a few tattered umbrellas for the girls to shield themselves from the sun.

Then the fat pig, weighing almost 200 pounds, came on board. This was the wedding gift from Carlo's grandparents. The pig stiffened his legs to keep from moving forward and squealed as the boys pushed and pulled him along the gangplank.

Peter and Osting tethered the pig's leg to the base of the mast to ensure that he did not slip while they sailed. His sad fate was to be roasted on a spit in the ground, lechon-baboy-style, and served in all his fatty glory as the highlight at the wedding reception.

Cooking a lechon was not a simple process. One needed to soak the pig meat in a special marinade for half a day, then stuff the pig with seasonings of lemon grass, garlic, anise, and onion. One then skewered the pig and roasted it in a charcoal-filled pit, turning it on the stick for several hours.

The basting coated onto the pig created a crisp, tasty skin. The savory meat was served along with plenty of tart coconut vinegar. No birthday party, village fiesta, or wedding was complete without serving a succulent lechon.

The men loaded the last sack on board as the six girls arrived with their bags and wedding presents. Parents, brothers, sisters, and neighbors shuffled barefoot along behind the girls like a slow parade. By now, Suluan had begun to wake up, and many had gathered along the beach out of pure curiosity.

As captain of his dad's boat for the day, Peter was eager to get out to sea with his friends. He smiled, let out a whistle, and waved to the girls to hurry into the boat. Carlo and Amado stood at the shore and relieved the girls of their luggage, handing it off to Roger, Jhun and Rey, who still balanced on the sagging plank.

Inside the sailboat, Mario, Domingo, and Alfredo

wrestled with a long, wet rope, which they attempted to untangle for Peter.

By this time, the intense reddish-orange ball of sun had crept up over the water's edge in the east and began its ascent for the day. However, large grayish clouds that hung low in the heavens covered most of the sun. Only small slivers of color peeked through between the dense clouds, and the massive ball looked like a prisoner trapped behind bars in its own sky.

Antonia looked across the crowd and caught a glimpse of Mam Salud's expression just as she shook her head and whispered something into Papa Beni's ear. Salud's all-seeing eye noticed something unsettling. She did not like the look of the eastern skyline, and neither did Papa Beni.

He shrugged his shoulders and wrinkled his brow, and then threw a quick, stern glance at his grandson Carlo, who worked diligently with the boys on the sailboat -- oblivious to the weather and the worried stares of his grandparents. Today the bridegroom had other things on his mind than the sky.

Why no one mentioned the signs in the sky on that fateful morning would be a question the people of Suluan would ask themselves for years to come.

Groups gathered to hug and kiss the young travelers good-bye and to cheer on Carlo and Daisy. The beach was flooded with activity and noise: children yelling, dogs yapping, roosters crowing, and concerned parents calling out last-minute instructions to their teens.

Nearby, someone on Suluan slaughtered a pig. Its pitifully piercing squeal rang louder than the other noise of the shoreline.

Antonia stood off to the side under a sprawling ipil-ipil tree, surrounded by a cluster of little children who clung to her hands and to the hem of her skirt. Everyone and everything seemed very other-worldly to her, as if she stood outside of this scene and looked down upon the beach.

Grim thoughts tripped over one another in her head.

Is this a dream? Is Carlo saying goodbye to Suluan… and to me forever?

The sky looked gloomy, and the air hung heavily around her.

Is Suluan itself grieving? Why is Mam Salud not smiling?

Her cousin Rosalyn, the youngest sister of Lita, tapped her on her thigh and reached up to hand Antonia a small, neatly-wrapped packet, pulling her favorite older cousin out of her trance-like stare.

Antonia stooped down, eye to eye with Rosalyn, who threw her arms tightly around Antonia's neck.

"What do you have for me, my little friend?"

"Open it! Open it!" Rosalyn said as she jumped up and down impatiently.

Inside the folded banana leaf was a brown leather string strung through a small hole in a pearly white shark's tooth. Antonia slipped it gently over her head and bent back down to scoop little Rosalyn up into her arms.

"Makain ka? Where are you going, Ate?"

"We are all going to Guiuan, Inday, to see manong Carlo marry Ate Daisy."

"Promise me you'll bring me something back from the other island," pleaded Rosalyn as she searched Antonia's black eyes.

"Oh, oh… yes! I promise to bring you lots of love back when I come," Antonia assured her little friend. "You'll see. I'll find you something wonderful. But Rosie, dear, I must go now. They are all waiting for me, and look, I'm again the last one! You run along, and I will see you next week when I return, okay?"

Always last.

Antonia hung her head and stared at the sand under her feet. She didn't like the uninvited feelings of self-pity mixed with anger that surged in behind the ugly phrase with all its lonely suggestions.

Rosalyn scampered back to her mother and shyly hid behind her legs, peeking out to wave good-bye only after the heavy-laden ship had pushed off to sea.

Peter, with the help of all the boys, hoisted the large white sail and positioned the boat so that it caught the morning wind. The fabric fluttered and whipped back and forth until the wind caught hold of it with a boom and blew the sailcloth taut like a drum.

Immediately the boat picked up speed; it jolted the group forward and partially knocked them off their feet. Everyone let out a shout, happy to finally be alone together and heading to Guiuan.

The teens regained their balance and hung on to one another as they waved back to shore where only a few parents stood at the water's edge. Antonia still saw her parents, Macaria and Bonifacio, who stood in the dim morning light, hand in hand alongside Mam Salud and Papa Beni.

To the far right stood the parents of Amado along with Bevs and Perla's families. Peter's father had found a stump a bit farther back from the water's edge where he could watch his son maneuver the ship. His hand was raised, and he still waved slowly.

The rest of the adults had returned to their breakfast duties and their many morning chores. The children went back to their games under the trees.

As they sailed out to sea, the sounds of barking dogs and crowing roosters grew faint, now replaced by the splash of water, the loud flap of the sailcloth, and the groan of the ship as it swayed.

Before them, the bow of the sailboat cut crisply through the crystal blue waves, which were unusually high and choppy this morning. Small whitecaps popped up here and there. The water was shallow and clear so that the teens could see through to the sandy bottom with its colorful life forms.

They saw scores of dazzling blue starfish, chunks of colorful coral, and schools of tiny fish who frantically dashed this way and that to avoid the stern of the boat. Leggy, brownish seaweed stretched upward as if to tickle the ocean surface with its toes; it swayed and quivered in the ripples and rings sent up by the undercurrents.

The boat sailed over groups of dark spiky sea anemones and precariously placed undersea rocks; the water was now deep enough that Peter no longer had to steer around the rocks.

Antonia had to squint her eyes as she looked down into the water. So much to see in the underworld. It's as if God hid these buried treasures and they're there to be discovered only by those who take the time to look.

She was one of those who wanted to see. Antonia occupied herself with the under-water world. It was a welcomed distraction from her pain and the desire to watch Carlo and Daisy.

It wasn't easy this morning. Antonia thought she'd best just watch the fish and push her feelings down under the waves. She headed toward the bow of the ship and bent over its edge to drag her hand just under the surface like a rudder.

The water was a soft and creamy blue. Mesmerized, she cut through the ripples with the edge of her hand like a knife through warm wax.

Salty sea spray splashed up Antonia's arm and whipped with moist, warmish wind onto her smiling face. Her hair blew freely round about, set free to fly like hundreds of thin wings flapping.

Everyone found a spot to drape either a leg or an arm over the side of the boat in order to feel the strength of the rushing water. Captain Peter stood erect, his dingy brown jacket tied tightly around his slim waist and a strip of tattered cloth wrapped low around his ruddy forehead. He looked like a true Spanish pirate of old who steered his vessel on the high seas.

Then, all of a sudden, the sailboat began to hop and to crash down hard. It struck and smacked the waves that came from every angle. The sailboat became increasingly strenuous for Peter to steer and difficult for his jarred passengers to ride.

A harsh, strident wind sharply blew into the sail. From where she sat near the bow, Antonia could no longer keep her hand in the water as the boat skipped and bounced higher and higher out of the water. Her face was wet from the spray. The sting of the suddenly unkind wind drove her to take a seat away from the rail.

She scooted carefully towards the center. Antonia sat close by Peter on one of the sun-bleached wooden planks that spanned the width of the ship. She breathed in the invigorating ocean air and closed her eyes tightly in a futile attempt to calm herself.

Her heart was beating fast. For the last twenty minutes, the waters had grown increasingly wild, and

Peter wrestled with the steering rod to keep the boat on course. Everyone else laughed and enjoyed the ride.

Antonia wrapped her arms around her waist and struggled to relax. She perched her bare feet on a sturdy-looking box in front of where she sat.

Everything is fine, Antonia thought, trying to soothe her anxiousness. *It's going to be fine. We are going to get there. I will not worry like my mom does.*

Her stomach was uneasy.

In an attempt to distract herself, she studied her friends and listened in to their chatter. Daisy and Carlo tried to keep each other balanced as the ship rocked. They stood shoulder to shoulder off to her right along the handrail towards the bow of the boat and stared in the direction where Guiuan would eventually come into view.

Rey, Jhun, Alfredo, and Domingo examined the fishing gear towards the rear of the boat. Nearby, Roger, Amado, and Mario laughed loudly as Amado entertained them with more of his storytelling.

The sea extended out endlessly before them without a trace of any island in sight. They had only been gone about half an hour, but to Antonia it seemed twice as long.

Perla saw Antonia seated in the middle of the boat, and she tiptoed unsteadily over the cargo in her direction. A warm smile spread across the two girls' faces as they sought the comfort of each other's company. Perla stretched out her arm around Antonia's shivering shoulders and drew her close. They spoke few words and focused their gaze first on the bow of the bouncing boat and then on Peter next to them as he struggled with the navigation.

The loud boys' antics drew the attention of all the girls as they made their way to the bow to join the others.

Perla leaned closer to Antonia and whispered, "Can

you keep a secret? I don't know if I should tell you or not. I may just be imagining this — but it kind of seems like, well, like Jhun spends a lot more time with me lately. He's really a nice guy, don't you think?"

"Perla! You finally notice him! I wondered how long it would take you," said Antonia.

"Aw, Tonya… are you just saying this to make me feel good? I hardly ever talk to Jhun."

"I know for a fact that he likes you. He even likes it that you are so quiet."

Perla began to open her heart and share about her year-long crush on Ofelia's brother, Jhun. She confessed her insecurities and fear of rejection. Antonia could not help but laugh, since she knew how much attention Jhun had paid Perla over the last few weeks — especially how much he had been at her side yesterday up at the cave. Perla was blind to his affection, and Antonia joked with her even more.

"You don't give enough credit to your own heart, Perla. Open your eyes a little more. Jhun has been at your side more times than you know. You play hard to get, and you don't even realize it. Good for you!"

Perla brushed her flying hair out of her face and grinned sheepishly.

"Do I? I am so sleepy," she told Antonia. "I'm going to just close my eyes for a while and get some rest."

Perla pulled up her legs and rested her forehead on her knees.

The wind around them picked up considerably. No one on board had any idea that this wind was about to take a turn for the worse. Before the storm hit, before the boat began to sink, before the teens were afloat at sea to fight for their lives, everyone felt carefree and happy.

CHAPTER SEVEN
THE STORM

Antonia subconsciously held her breath and studied the unsettled tropical sky. Warily, she peered in every direction. Perla hunched over next to her on the wooden bench. Perla, who'd been up long before dawn, rested her head on folded, pale brown arms. It wasn't long before the steady up-and-down movement of the lengthy sailboat rocked her to sleep.

Antonia risked another glance at the sky and turned nonchalantly back toward her beloved Suluan, where she had seen the evil intruder high in the sky the day before. What she feared was creeping upon them.

The big rising ball of sun she had seen at the shoreline this morning when they set sail was nowhere in sight. It was gone, incarcerated somewhere beyond the heavily hung clouds. Instead, monstrous and ominous gray forms groped their way across the heavens at a quick pace, chasing the sailboat with angry ferocity.

"Oh no, this can't be happening," whispered Antonia, turning back to see if her fourteen other friends had noticed the impending storm.

They hadn't. Not yet. Her forehead furrowed and her eyes brimmed with tears; she glanced up to observe Peter. At the helm, Peter threw Antonia a worried glance and grabbed the long wooden tiller. He jerked it roughly back and forth. He'd wrestled with the sailboat for the past twenty minutes or more.

His knuckles were now white, and his teeth clenched as he struggled to keep the boat and himself upright and on course. He angled the bow to cut through the waves to keep it from tipping over. Peter shook; his eyes wide with fear.

No one else on board had taken note of the ever-darkening sky. Everyone continued to joke and laugh. All the teens stood together near the bow of the ship with their backs to the impending storm.

The boys were showing off, of course, just as they had yesterday at the cave. They struggled to balance themselves and rode the boat as if they were riding bulls at a rodeo. The girls laughed, forgetting the condition of their hair as the water splashed up and covered them with salty spray.

Her best friends from Suluan braved the elements with occasional girlish squeals. Bevs, Ofelia, and Lita stood close together, bound with arms wrapped around one another's waist. They leaned far out over the edge like a bow ornament on a grand ship.

Antonia recalled pictures she had seen of carved sculptures imbuing the bows of early sailing ships: golden-haired figureheads dressed in flowing gowns, mermaids, twin sisters, and mariners perched at their nautical posts.

A poem her class had to memorize at school raced into her thoughts: "And there's many a story that could be told, of the fine figure-heads that were chiseled of old. On the dreary sands they crumble today, from Terra del Fuego to Baffins Bay."

Antonia shivered and wiped her eyes. The rowdy laughter of the boys increased as the ship pounded harder on each new wave.

What was it we learned at school about those Greek myths and ancient legends?

She tried to remember. Her teacher had told the class that sailors often adorned the prows of their galleys with a beautiful wooden woman, who was believed to possess an ability to calm Neptune, the so-called god of the sea.

Battling the wind, the sculpture supposedly embodied the spirit of the sailing ship as she looked down over the waves. She made sure the voyage would be safe by soothing the sea gods.

Hopefully we'll safely reach Guiuan today, Antonia told herself, but she was skeptical.

She looked up at the dismal sky and again to her happy friends. The three young ladies entwined together at the front of the sailing boat rocked unsteadily from side to side and giggled. They told secrets in whispers; their hair, black and not golden, whipping wildly in the wind.

Her friends held one another upright as the boat bounced higher and higher. Antonia had to laugh at their failed attempts to stay standing.

She turned her gaze a few feet to the right of this group, where Carlo and Daisy stood shoulder to shoulder. The soon-to-be-married couple swayed together with the rhythm of the bouncing boat, oblivious to all else.

Thoughts of tomorrow's wedding and of a new life together filled their minds. Antonia's smile disappeared as she fought against her own jealous thoughts.

Who will calm the storm in my heart?

She watched Carlo joke with charming Daisy. In an effort to refocus, she bit her lower lip and shifted her gaze back to the giggling threesome, then up to the heavens.

The girls' laughter turned to shrieks as ocean water splashed high overboard to envelope them. The wind kicked up and transformed into an instant tempest. The strong gusts whined slow and long like a high-pitched train whistle. Enormous waves roared over the side of the sailboat and sloshed underfoot.

As if on cue, the group of friends turned around simultaneously. With wide eyes and mouths agape, their laughter turned to fear as awareness of the storm crested over each youth like a wave. They looked back and forth between Peter and the rude black sky now completely overshadowing them.

"What's going on?" yelled Bevs. She hunched over as if to hide from the approaching storm.

"Where did *this* storm come from all of a sudden?" Mario screamed and shook his head in disbelief.

He raised an angry fist heavenward.

"It's a typhoon! I'm scared!" said Ofelia, as she buried her head in her brother Jhun's wet shoulder.

Ofelia began to cry.

Every fisherman's son in the Philippines knew that a storm at sea could arrive without warning. The air felt electric. The wind smelled sour, like rotten seaweed.

Instinctively, the boys grabbed the girls and pulled them toward the center of the boat, where Antonia and a now wide-awake Perla crouched together.

The boat bounced up, down, and in every direction, as small in the towering waves as a grain of Suluan sand. The unpredictable jolts threw the youths to the wet floorboards of the sailboat. The crash and roar of the ocean covered their desperate screams for help.

From the top of every crest, Antonia could see the waves grow bigger and blacker all around. The wind rose and the boat surrendered to the sea. When it dropped down, the massive waves rose up around it with twenty-foot walls of solid water.

Secure within the crusty walls of the cave on Suluan

yesterday, Antonia had been safe. Here, she was in peril. At one moment, the waves completely encompassed them, and the next moment the boat rose again and was on top.

Frightened beyond words, the teens huddled closer together and grabbed on to the boxes and bags surrounding them. Everything else slid. Helplessly tethered to the mast, the fat pig lay wet on his side and squealed in terror. The chickens, trapped in their make-shift cages, squawked and flew on top of each other.

The sky unzipped, and rain fell in sheets and torrents. Antonia's stomach was uneasy. A deep, ominous rumbling filled the air, like the sound of drums echoing in a cavern. Lightning flashed, and a boisterous boom of thunder seemed to break the sky in two just over their heads.

Wave after wave rose up before them, beside them, behind them as if they were nothing to the great swells. Suddenly, the mast shattered with a deafening crack, and wood splintered in every direction. The white sail ripped apart, and the halves flapped and tangled among flying ropes and flailing wet arms.

The heavy, drenched cloth wrapped around Peter's upper torso and face until he disappeared into a ghostly mass. As he attempted to wrestle himself free, he lost his grip of the rudder and thus the command of the ship.

Another wave hit, and Peter lost his footing. Antonia watched as he came crashing down on top of Mario, who had been crouching next to her. All semblance of order disappeared. The friends cried out in anguish as the storm jerked away the last of their control.

The boat was at the mercy of the angry waves. Tossed like a tiny piece of drift-wood, the sailboat rapidly filled with water. An eerie stillness came in between the peals of thunder and bursts of rain.

During a lull in the storm, Roger grabbed the bucket next to him and tried his best to bail out the ankle-deep water rising on the floorboards. But every wave sent him tripping and tumbling again to the ground.

The sky was a roof of dark, sinister black. No longer could the teens see the pale blue-gray, which had covered them for the past hour. Icy rain lashed upon them as they rode the crown of yet another gigantic wave and then wallowed in the cavernous trough of a new one. The wind, which had begun as a soft slow whistle, increased to a moaning wail over the waves, like a grisly wounded animal.

As the keel boomed against the force of the sea beneath, waves slapped the youths within the ship. Cold, gloomy seawater spilled down their necks, freezing and blinding them.

"Antonia, help!" yelled Perla, "We're all going to die!"

A bolt of lightning flashed above the ship. Perla curled up in a ball and shivered violently. Antonia could barely hear her tiny voice over the clamor of the sea and the tumult in the ship; even the air itself was screaming.

Antonia raised her voice above the din and reached out to hug Perla's shaking body.

"Perla...just hang on. We're together. You'll see! We'll get out of this. Do not give up!"

The full force of a typhoon was upon them. It grew more difficult to hold on to the boat and one another as they squatted on the slippery floor. Waves relentlessly splashed over the entire boat. The sea was gulping thirstily at them, longing to swallow them whole.

If only I could see something besides black waves! Antonia lifted her rain-drenched face to the heavens. *Oh, God, help us! This storm won't last long. At least, I hope it won't.*

Another bolt of lightning split the sky, and Antonia jerked and ducked her head.

They were at war with the sea, and more: the sea, the clouds, and the wind had all declared war on them! Who were *they*? Only fifteen teenagers. And throughout history, the strong forces of nature had seldom lost a battle.

A force underneath the waters rose angrily from the port side of the boat, tilting it to a 60-degree angle. What was left of the broken mast dipped farther and farther toward the right side. Then a solid mountainous wall of water hit them broadside, obscuring everything.

The vicious storm tore the group of dear friends from the island of Suluan apart. They lost their tight hold on one another, slipped and slid in every direction, and collided into the loosened cargo and the sides of the ship.

Bevs crawled on her hands and knees back to the center of the ship and clung to Lita and Ofelia. The girls wept. Another huge wave splashed in and out of the ship, and with it the three friends were carried together over the edge and disappeared into the turbulent ocean.

The boat hung suspended on its side for a moment that stretched as wide as the sea and then with the onslaught of yet another angered wave, it filled with more water, tipped back, and returned to its sailing position, only to begin sinking. The weight of the waves pulled the boat down as the people and packages that had been crammed inside floated up out of it.

Arms and legs flailed everywhere, now tangled in a chaotic fight for survival amidst cries of anguish. Ropes floated like twisted snakes between boxes and buckets on the waves.

The sea held the submerged boat in its iron-fisted grip as its former passengers, now pounded by the savage waters, struggled in terror to find one another.

Gasping for air, Antonia struggled to orient herself in

the mayhem. Pelting rain, continuous booms of thunder and shouts for help surrounded and terrified her, sapping her strength. The stormy water was ice cold.

"Where is everyone? What do we do now? How do we get help?" Antonia sobbed her questions into the vicious wind. "Get back to the boat, back to the boat, back to the boat," she chanted aloud. Her self-talk propelled her to search the debilitating darkness for something to hold.

The foaming sea first shoved the teens into one another, then ripped them far apart. The waves lifted them up together and threw them down without a care. They grabbed on to nameless shoulders, necks, legs -- whatever came close to them in the darkness.

A second later, another wave angrily ambushed them. Separated, alone, and lost, each struggled to survive. Like impenetrable walls, the sardonic waves rose up between the friends from Suluan.

Around them floated boxes of wedding presents, sacks of food, the partially sunken crate of a dozen chickens -- now all drowned and quiet. Belly side up, the pig was silent.

Through the darkness and the heavy sheets of rain, Antonia caught a glimpse of the broken mast, which now stood out as a lone wounded survivor -- an obscure silhouetted focal point. The young Filipina fought her way through the churning water. She grappled toward the ship's stern and grabbed hold of it.

Antonia rose and fell with the underwater boat, but it gave her a chance to catch her breath and look for her friends.

My friends! Where is Carlo? What happened to Ofelia and Lita? And my Bevs? She can't swim. Where is she? Where are all the boys -- I don't see anyone!

She heard muffled calls for help from all sides, but she was unable to see or hear clearly due to the turbulent waves and pounding rain. The salt stung her eyes and filled her nose and mouth. Antonia found it difficult to hang on to the slippery wood.

Sticks, seaweed, ropes, tarp from the sail, food -- her hundreds of neatly wrapped spring rolls -- palm leaves, and wedding presents floated all around her. With a swift kick, Antonia pushed away a box coming straight at her.

"Bevs! Bevs....come here to me! Here's the boat! Hey... over *here*!"

Antonia's loud cries rang out like a muffled bell amid the winds that howled.

High up in the cave yesterday, Bevs had laid her head on Antonia's lap, and today she was struggling to keep her head above water!

Luckily, the wooden wreckage remained buoyant, although it now floated under the waves. Whether because they heard Antonia, or saw the mast for themselves, the friends began streaming in to the relative safety of the wreck.

Daisy arrived first with Bevs on her back. Full of panic, Bevs clutched her friend's long hair and hung on for dear life. The young people surfaced and fought their way to the destroyed ship. Everyone latched onto an edge, a pole, or a jutting piece of broken wood still attached to the hull.

There were few words spoken, just loud sighs of relief and sobs as each one seized someone or something to keep his or her head above water.

Carlo shouted out all the names and searched for the familiar faces of his childhood friends, these sons of fishermen, these princes of the sea.

"Rey. Roger. Mario. Domingo. Alfredo. Jhun. Peter. Amado."

His voice was shaky yet still strong and full of manly authority. The burly wind whipped his face as he glanced around for the girls and continued to shout.

"Daisy. Tonya. Bevs!…….. Ofelia. Lita…uh…ahh… Perla. Hey girls! *Girls!*"

He strained to find the fourteen heads of his teenage friends, which barely peeked out from above the water's surface.

"You're all here! Salamat sa Ginoo! Thank God!"

They were all alive, at least for now.

His voice sounded relieved, but his eyes looked wild and frantic. He exuded a sense of responsibility for this wedding crew, who now wrestled for their lives in the middle of a killer typhoon. His upcoming wedding with Daisy was the reason why they all left Suluan only to land out here in the deep. It was all because of him.

The incessant rain blew from every direction and slapped their faces. The ocean heaved higher and higher. Antonia could not think straight. Carlo's strong voice and the sight of her friends all alive helped her focus a bit.

In her heart, she begged God for help, for rescue, for some miracle in the middle of this squall. All she wanted was the solid ground of Suluan. Here, she could not reach the bottom.

Some school of fish we are. We are no match for this storm. What do we do now? Where can we go?

Her mind raced back to the circle of hand-holding friends eating their last supper within the confines of the quiet cave. Then she thought of the coolness of her mother's hand and her last tender words to her early that morning -- to be strong.

How can I be strong in the middle of a typhoon out at sea? What if there are sharks here -- right here where we are!

Once, a shark had ripped the skin off a well-loved fisherman's back so deep that his lungs were exposed. By the time his companions rescued him, the fisherman had lost an arm. Who would pull her and her friends to safety if sharks encircled them? She pulled her knees up to her chest.

Just yesterday, Antonia and her friends had gathered at their hide-away cave for a farewell party. The girls had talked of marriage. The boys had played like pirates up at the lighthouse. They had all slept peacefully with their families in their simple huts.

Who would have thought that they would be fighting for their lives in a typhoon mere hours later? They were on their way to a wedding! This was supposed to be a dream week. Now it was a nightmare.

CHAPTER EIGHT
THE RESCUE

Antonia looked around for Perla and saw that Jhun held her up under her frail shoulders. Perla was not a strong swimmer. Like so many of the island children, she had played in the water every day but never learned to swim properly.

Jhun encouraged her to hang on to a rope they had found still attached to the broken mast. Antonia's eyes met Perla's, and Perla shook her head and looked down.

Rey, whose wide smile normally lifted everyone's mood, was serious and somber. His typical positive style of communication brazenly shifted to one of a commanding military officer. He lifted his voice so that all could hear.

"We need to all hang on together and ride out this storm. We may have to spend the whole day, and maybe even the night here. But as soon as it lets up, I think we men should swim back for help."

This was the first glimmer of hope Antonia had felt as she surveyed all her beautiful Filipina friends. They now tread water and clung to one another and the capsized ship. She wondered if they could hold on much longer. The typhoon was still upon them. They clustered tightly together, shivering from the cold and the shock. Lita cried uncontrollably while the boys around her desperately tried to comfort her.

"Just hold on, Lit," they shouted in unison.

Carlo yelled into the storm, "Come on, we have to make it! We can't lose each other, not like this, not here. Everybody hold on tight," he said, his eyes filling with tears.

Another huge wave crashed over their heads and sucked them down under its force. Up again they rose and sputtered; they fought to breathe while grabbing whatever piece of the floating broken ship they could find.

This scene repeated itself incessantly for the next several hours. Frightened and exhausted from the battle, the comrades took turns pulling one another up out of the frigid water onto the remains of the boat.

As Rey had guessed, the storm raged on into the night hours, and the teens fought fatigue as much as they struggled against the typhoon.

The greatest enemy they faced, though, was the overpowering sense of dread within. The threat of drowning, giving in to the cold, or falling prey to the sharks that roamed the Pacific tormented each mind.

Morning came as a welcome and long-awaited guest. An insipidly pale sky peeked through the dingy heavens between a slight break in the clouds. The storm wind still blew steadily, and the waves rose and fell intensely -- but there was light, and the rain had stopped sometime in the middle of the night.

The light gave no warmth to the day; it cast a queer greenish-yellow light that made the horizon look sickly as the day slowly unfolded over the sea.

Soggy packets of Antonia's homemade spring rolls and clusters of hanging rice bags bobbed around them. Roger gathered the food and passed it out among his friends.

"Eat these," he urged as he tossed the wet food to everyone. "We all need our strength for today. It's all we have right now."

They unwrapped the spring rolls and squeezed the brackish water out. It was not such a breakfast as they would have chosen, for the boys dreamt of hot rice, fried eggs and fish, and the girls for hot native chocolate and warm rolls, but it would suffice. From the way they devoured the mushy meal, anyone would have supposed it was delicious.

Antonia's fingers were so cold and stiff that she could not quite undo the tight weave of the little rice sack. Bevs noticed her friend struggling and used her teeth to rip open the sack for her. Maybe this bit of food would help calm Antonia's queasy stomach.

The boys began planning their swim back to Suluan for help. They would use boards from the boat as floatation devices so that they could hang onto the boards and kick their way home.

The boys struggled to wrench planks free from the shattered ship's hull while treading water. They secured three long boards they could share among the nine of them.

"Yeah," said Amado, as he sputtered saltwater out of his mouth. "That's right, yank these boards free. We can paddle our way back home now that the storm has let up."

Carlo added, "You girls stay here together, and you'll be safe until help comes."

It had taken an hour by boat to get this far. However, the storm had also blown them off course, so the young men were a bit unsure about where they were and how long it might take them to reach their island again.

No landmarks were in sight, just endless, nonstop

waves. The dim morning light that increased in the eastern skies gave them a better sense of direction.

"I hope the storm doesn't start up again," yelled Carlo to the boys.

Amado swam over to where Carlo was in the water.

"Right. We need to go now and get a head start just in case it whips back around. If it starts to rain again, it's gonna be impossible to see where we need to swim.," said Amado.

The six girls moved closer to one another. Their sea-soaked clothing clung uncomfortably to their skin like cold glue. It was hard not to cry as they looked out at their brave friends about to embark on this dangerous rescue mission.

Moreover, they knew that alone at sea, they might face a new storm by themselves or something worse, like undertows -- or sharks!

How long must we float alone...wait alone? Antonia thought. *I want to go home.*

She summoned every bit of inner strength she had and forced a weak smile while she looked each girl in the eye. She hoped to raise their level of confidence... or at least push away their apprehension as the boys prepared to leave them. No one spoke much.

Antonia and Daisy's eyes met, and Daisy returned a weary smile but without the normal twinkle in her eyes. She had desperately tried to gather her wedding presents floating all around her, but she'd failed.

The thought that her fiancée was soon to disappear among the waves just a day before their planned wedding was almost too much to bear.

Antonia felt her friend's torment. She had never seen Daisy so distraught. Antonia lowered her eyes and began to weep.

She knew all too well that the boys' chances of

swimming back to Suluan during a typhoon were slim. She admired their courage but struggled to let them go. She longed to speak words of faith and hope to the group, but she was not sure she could handle saying even a timid "good-bye".

Everything in her wanted to cry out and beg them to stay, but she dared not express her fears to the young men or the girls. No, she must trust. Perhaps rescue was actually possible.

Filipinos taught their children not to show affection in public, but since no adults were present to scold them, there was no reason to follow this rule right now. An engaged couple was about to endure the worst trial of their young love.

Carlo swam to Daisy, and in full view of all thirteen friends, he held her in his strong arms and kissed her passionately.

Ashamed, the others turned their heads or closed their eyes, afraid of trespassing on a sacred moment. The whistling wind carried the muffled sobs of the sweethearts into the distance. Daisy clung to Carlo until he pulled her arms from his neck. He wiped his face and whispered farewell.

The boys shouted their "good-byes" to the girls with a stronger tone in their voices and wished them well. They grabbed their planks and motored their way toward the strange eastern sky, leaving the girls with a last view of kicking legs that cut in and out of the undulating waves

Fishing and swimming came naturally to all of the boys -- all of them, that is, except Roger, who had never learned to swim. But his legs were the longest and the strongest, so he hung on to the board and kicked like crazy with the others.

These fishermen's sons had spent as much time in

boats as they had on land while growing up. Nothing, however, could have prepared them for the hours that stretched before them, because the storm was not over, and the wind and waves resisted their efforts.

Magellan himself would have been proud of these valiant sailors, who, like his crew, dared to tackle the untamed Pacific in search of land. Mario, more than anyone, knew all too well the fate of the Spanish explorers. The story he had told just two days ago relentlessly drummed in his brain, mocking his heroic rescue efforts.

With every splash of a new wave, he fought his own terror-filled thoughts of drowning at sea or worse: being torn apart by ferocious sharks.

Hours passed, and the rain began to fall again from a jealous sky. At first, a few large drops trickled down, and then the cloaked heavens unleashed a shower of painful daggers that stung the boys' backs as they paddled eastward. It was impossible to ignore the storm, and their arms and legs ached, but no one complained.

No one mentioned the girls. No one talked about sharks. No one wanted to drink the bitter water of defeat.

"Where are Jonah and his whale now when we need him?" Carlo talked to himself as he closed his eyes.

The tale of Jonah was the first sermon he had ever heard as a young boy in the Catholic Church he attended while going to school in Guiuan. Memories of stained glass windows, the pungent scent of incense, the flowing white robes of the priests, and a liturgical mass spoken in strange Latin words flooded his mind.

He had knelt on a wooden pew and felt the awe of the holy chapel as a child. Now the thought of the chapel brought him peace in the middle of this storm.

"Right about now we could use a huge rescuer -- someone or something to save us," he said under his breath.

He thought of Daisy, of all the girls, of Tonya -- his childhood comrade -- and then he thought of possible sharks lurking below the waves, and he kicked harder.

The shark-infested waters around Suluan had proven dangerous as far back as he could remember. Men caught unaware, spear fishing in waist-deep water, had had their thighs ripped open without seeing the slightest shadow or ripple beforehand.

Flanking him were the two brothers, Domingo and Alfredo. They huffed and strained to continue. Despite their muscular physique and youthful potency, they were in pain and slowed down.

But no one gave voice to the agony inside him. It was like running up the steps to the lighthouse: they knew to ignore their own aching torment.

A sickly unrest swirled in the air. Mixed with the pelting rain, the strange tone of the sky, and the turbulent water, the atmosphere weakened the boys' resistance. The enormity of their task began to gnaw away at their confidence. Hope lost its anchor in their soul, and several of the boys slipped from their piece of wood each time a new wave hit them.

Frail calls for help came first from one boy, then from another. Roger lost his grip after a huge wave hit him from the side, and he flailed in the water. Since he did not know how to swim, his attempts to keep his head above water were unsuccessful.

A strong undercurrent sucked his large frame down out of sight. He disappeared. Mario and Jhun, who had been together with him a moment before, jerked around to search for him in the dark sea. The two scanned the water frantically. There was no sign of him, just more waves, more rain, more wind.

Roger had drowned.

With loud, heartbreaking sobs, the boys called out to the remaining six with the sad news. The dismal reality hit the others hard, and they, too, began to weep together, their salty tears mixing with the salty sea. Roger, their big gentle friend, was gone forever.

The news of Roger slipping into the sea shattered what little strength the boys had left. Their kicking slowed down and became irregular. They avoided one another's worried glances, and their heads were heavy.

Mario shook violently, unable to overcome the anguish that gripped him; torment like a steel vice froze his muscles and held him captive. He could no longer kick his heavy legs. His thoughts began to race, his heart beat wildly, and panic filled him.

Beside him, Jhun could sense Mario's tension and his mounting moans of distress. He reached out to touch his shoulder with his one hand, while he struggled to hang on with the other. Then something in Mario snapped, and blood-curdling screams erupted from deep within his soul.

They scared Jhun.

"Bro... Mario... it's ok. Come on; we're gonna make it," said Jhun, his voice quivering. "Think of our families; they are waiting for us — let's keep kicking, and we'll get there together."

But Mario could not be comforted. He lost his grip, slipping off the board when the next wave hit and sliding under the water with a pitiful cry of defeat. Jhun bravely dove down, though he could not see anything, and grabbed around under the ocean's surface. He groped his hands wildly through the empty water.

But Mario was gone, with the ocean for his grave.

Who will be next?

Jhun shuddered to think as he once again took hold of his floating plank of wood.

He thought about yesterday morning, when he had challenged his friends to charge up the lighthouse steps in the heat of the day. Racing against each other -- trying to be first.

Now look at us. We're all last. We just lost Mario. It was Mario who told us those stories about Magellan. Mar's gone....

Fear drove the young men to continue; there was no turning back and no other choice but to persist, to fight, and to endure. This long and painful battle with nature seemed to have no end in sight.

After all this effort of kicking, there was still no land in view, no familiar landmark by which the boys could orient themselves, no lighthouse to guide their way.

Fatigue slowed them down, as did the steady wind and rain constantly assaulting them.

CHAPTER NINE
THE RETURN

The boys pressed on slowly but surely. All seven boys stayed in closer proximity to one another since losing Roger and Mario. Rey swam over to Jhun to keep him company on his board so that he would not have to fight the waves alone. Amado and Peter came together, shoulder to shoulder, and that sparked a new determination to stay afloat.

Echoes of the winds whipped about them for hours. Finally, they grew hoarse from singing their drawn-out dirge. Alfredo thought he saw the faint grayish blur of land in the distance.

"Look!" he shouted to the others. "Look over there to the right!"

Sure enough, when the waves lifted them out from the deep troughs of the sea, they saw a familiar protruding rock on the horizon. Its indistinct tree shapes thrust their crowning palms into the sky like umbrellas. It was not Suluan, but they knew this place well.

Adrenaline shot through the boys like fire, and its combustion drove them ahead with a new spark of hope. As they neared the beachhead, the gangly trees waved a welcome to come ashore. This was the small, uninhabited island, no longer than three ship lengths, that the boys had wanted to visit on their way to Guiuan to hunt for crabs.

Bone weary, they barely crawled up out of the wild surf and on to the cream-colored beach strewn with broken branches, huge palm leaves, pungent seaweed, and driftwood blown in from the typhoon. The seven boys lay sprawled close to one another on the cold seashore. They shivered uncontrollably, exhausted.

None of the boys had drunk any water since they had left Suluan, and they were severely dehydrated. Two days ago they had raised their coconuts in a loud toast to Magellan. Right now their voices were silenced as they struggled to stay alive.

Carlo weakly propped himself up on his elbows and surveyed his waterlogged companions who heaved, coughed, and moaned from extreme fatigue. Their clothes were torn, their hair wild as lightning.

For several minutes, no one spoke a word. Domingo had a crazed look in his eyes and choked back deep sobs. Alfredo lay still with his face down and buried in his hands. Rey and Jhun were curled up in a fetal position close to each other. Peter lay on his back and stared with empty eyes at the clouds.

Amado rose to his knees, brushed sand off his body, and looked around, bewildered. Carlo was at a loss for words. He buried his face in his swollen hands and wept loudly.

By now, it was late in the afternoon, which meant that they had swum in the stormy sea for many hours since leaving the girls as the sun rose.

"Perhaps," Carlo said, "we've been kicking for the last nine hours or more. What in the world should we do now?" *We can't stay here tonight,* he thought to himself. *There is no water, no shelter…and we must get help for the girls.*

He sat up, wiped his eyes, and hung his waterlogged head. Thoughts of Daisy filled his heart.

Amado crawled over to Carlo and laid his heavy arm across his best friend's back.

"Hey, bai, when do you think we should start swimming again?"

"Yeah, I was just thinking the same thing. The sooner the better," answered Carlo.

"We have to rescue the girls," Amado said to his friend.

Neither of the two could stand, as their legs were wobbly and weak. The boys felt nauseous and dizzy. Instead of walking, Carlo and Amado laboriously and painfully crawled over the sand to sit closer to their friends.

"Ok, men," said Carlo, "we have to think of the girls alone out there in the sea, and we need to get back in the water and head home. The way I figure it, the sky looks calmer than before, the waves aren't so wild, and I think we can reach Suluan in two hours or so."

Alfredo rolled on his back with a loud groan.

"You're right, Carlo... but... " Alfredo's voice cracked and faded to nothing.

He already knew the answer. Everyone knew that this was not the end of their journey, nor could they waste another minute talking about how tired they were -- or how scared.

Amado stood slowly like an old, crippled man looking out to sea. He had drawn himself up to his last frail inch.

"Come on, everybody. Let's grab our boards and ride those waves home for help. We're losing precious time the longer we sit here."

"I... I... I... d-d-d-don't... k-k-k-know... if I can m-m-m-make it," Domingo said.

There was a pause so long that the boys began to wonder if Carlo -- or anyone else, for that matter -- would say anything. When Carlo did speak, it was in a lower voice, as if he himself did not much like what he was saying.

"After all we've been through in the last two days, I don't blame anyone for being scared or tired... or wanting to rest, but... " he paused and looked up at the sky in an attempt to read the air. "It's the girls; I just don't know how long they can all hang on. That water is colder now, and the wind is still... still very strong. And I am worried that the sharks... " His voice cracked and faded.

Jhun snapped in anger, "We lost Roger and Mario! I couldn't find Mario in the waves... he -- he -- he just disappeared right next to me. I could have saved him, but I lost him."

"And... Roger couldn't swim at all; we all knew that. We really didn't have any other choice, and we can't give up now," Amado said in a raspy voice.

More silence.

Painstakingly, they helped one another up and hesitantly faced the wide sea together. They stood like old soldiers about to enter their next battle. Every muscle ached, and their legs felt like rubber. Their brown skin had a whitish crust on it from the salt water. They were chilled and shook violently.

Peter spoke up softly.

"Hey guys, there is so much more to our lives than what we see right now — we've got our whole lives ahead of us." He paused and swallowed hard. "I have to get home to my father."

Another long pause.

He continued, "And... we've got to all dance at kuya Carlo's wedding."

All the boys laughed. The joke helped break their fear about getting back in the water.

"You know we Filipinos, we're like bamboo. We bend with the wind, but we can survive the storm," Amado said. "Right now we are all pretty bent, but we will survive."

Struggling, Carlo lifted Domingo off the ground with a big bear hug.

"My buddy! Come on, Doming. We'll do this together and get home to see our families and then go out to save the girls. Ok?"

Domingo grunted and looked away.

Shaken by the deaths of his two friends, fear controlled Domingo's movements, making them stiff and slow.

Rain began to fall gently on the boys as they picked up their broken boards and took off to swim towards Suluan. Hours passed, and the rain continued to fall steadily. Just as the boys thought they could kick no more, they saw a shadow arise in the distance. They knew it was Suluan!

This hope spurred them all on, except for Domingo. He began to panic and to cry loudly. Carlo, who hung on next to him, tried his best to speak encouraging words to him and even scolded him at one point.

Nothing seemed to help Domingo snap out of his ranting. He was having a breakdown right then, just as they had sight of the shore.

Domingo slowed down and loosened his grasp of the floating board. Repeatedly, Carlo and Alfredo yanked him back; each time, he slipped behind, even though they also struggled with their own extreme exhaustion.

Then it happened: Domingo completely stiffened. His hands froze like stone, and he stopped kicking all together. He gulped in water, choked, and sank under the dark, rough waters.

"Doming, noooo!" screamed Carlo and Alfredo together as they fought with the waves to reach out and rescue him.

They dove underneath the water and fervently pursued his body, which descended like a sinking ship, pulled down by powerful currents. Alfredo caught his brother's wrist and pulled as hard as he could as he struggled to kick his way back to the surface for air.

Just as he reached the surface, Doming's wrist slipped from Alfredo's grip. Alfredo came up, gasped for air, and returned down to retrieve his brother once again.

Carlo was right by him this time, and the two thrashed wildly and chased after Domingo. With the next big wave, Domingo disappeared out of sight; the heartless undertow of the sea sucked him shamelessly out to his grave. The two returned to the surface with angry, bursting lungs.

"No! No! No! Not Doming," wailed Alfredo as he banged his fist on the floating board in front of him.

Carlo struggled to breathe and looked with pity at his grieving friend. He began to reckon with the fact that they were about to face villagers who were missing their children. A badge of shame rather than a badge of courage was painfully pinned to his soul.

We left with fifteen, and we return now with only six. What will we tell everyone? How will we ever find the girls?

His mind raced out of control as he searched the shoreline. Carlo shook with anger and exhaustion. It was then that he realized the depth of his tiredness. Gradually their feet touched the sandy bottom, and although their will to reach dry ground had climaxed, their strength to fight even the smallest of waves failed. They dragged their rubbery legs like weights against the resistance of the sea, barely moving forward.

Several fishermen who were crouched under a tree on the shore, deep in conversation, spotted the boys as they struggled to walk through the turbulent surf. The men shouted to the village for help. Soon a hundred men, women, and children encompassed the stumbling young men in the water. Their boys had made it home.

As the evening light faded into dusk, six strong men carried the half-drowned boys to shore and immediately wrapped them in blankets, though a million blankets could not have warmed the boys at this point. Each family withdrew with their precious son into their home, followed by an entourage of anxious relatives, friends, and neighbors.

The women set to work cooking hot rice porridge and fish soup for the boys. The men built fires; the children ran to gather sticks and wood. The village of Suluan wept.

The families of the six girls and the missing three boys stood in the rain huddled close together at the shore and looked desperately out to sea. All they knew about their missing children was what came from a groom-to-be who whispered while he wept.

"The girls are waiting for us -- they're all alone -- I'm afraid of the currents, and..." he paused, "of sharks."

Carlo did not care that they saw him cry.

Night fell fast over Suluan.

The young men all hung on to life and shook uncontrollably; some of them vomited, and some convulsed. Jhun suffered the most at this point. Fever wracked his body as he drifted in and out of consciousness.

Rey lay stiffly still, no longer able to talk. Peter's father rocked his swaddled son like a small child and spoke gently to calm his wordless moans.

Alfredo could not hold back his sobs as he slowly recounted the agonizing death of his brother moments before they reached the shore. The loss of Domingo had crushed his young heart. His family crowded closely around him in mournful stillness.

The big family of Amado sat vigil at his bedside as he slept a fitful sleep. There was nothing they could do but to sit and keep watch over his restless, twitching body. The overwhelming trek back to Suluan had sucked the joyful life of out of Amado.

But the home of Papa Beni and Mam Salud was busy. Carlo sat hunched over and weak, wrapped in old blankets from his head down to his lower legs. He trembled and wept silently, mostly unable to speak, and when he did, he could answer only a few of the well-meant questions thrown at him.

Tearfully, he told of the half-sunken boat and the deaths of Roger, Mario, and Doming. His swollen, ice-cold feet soaked in an old wooden basin of hot water that Papa Beni changed every fifteen minutes.

His head throbbed hard, his queasy stomach ached, and his inflamed eyes shut, still burning from the salt.

Mam Salud stood with her arms crossed in a far corner of the living room and spoke in hushed tones with several of the village leaders far enough away that Carlo could not hear them.

The men discussed whether they should leave immediately to find the girls or wait until the winds died down. Unfortunately, the sailboat of Peter's father was no longer available to them, and most of the men doubted that their smaller fishing boats would be sturdy enough to tackle the still-raging sea.

"What are we going to do?" said Osting.

They turned to Salud for answers, their faces sober. They read her answer in silence.

Of course they all knew the route to Guiuan like the back of their leathery fishermen hands, but they were unsure if in the dark they could locate the girls. Against all good reason, but driven by the love of fathers, they decided to set out to sea in two boats to search for the girls. Not a whisper challenged them.

"Take all the lanterns and ropes you have," Beni said. "We'll start now and try to find where the boat has capsized -- and if --" he hesitated, feeling awkward but compelled to speak. "If there are signs of possible survival, we'll search every inch of the sea until we find them."

The men were silent, no one questioning his command.

Solemn on-lookers gathered at the shore as a group of eight men pushed out into the rough waters. The sun sank in a dismally apathetic western sky. The parents of Suluan waited in the darkness, making no sound. One by one, others from the island came to the shoreline.

Five hours later, the defeated fathers returned home with heavy hearts to a desolate, dark beach. They brought with them nothing but a silent question:

What has happened to our girls?

CHAPTER TEN
THE CURRENTS

It wasn't long after the boys had swum out of sight that the girls moved as well, tugged farther out to sea by strong currents. Antonia clung to her corner of the floating ship just as she had clung to her home in Suluan.

The rain pelted them mercilessly. They hung on to the mast of the sunken vessel and to one another as best they could. Each fought her personal inward battle against a foe of unrelenting terror. Dread demonized each girl with the arrival of every angry, demanding wave.

The struggle just to hold on became ever more wearisome as the hours passed. Every recurring surge of the sea seemed like an enemy sent to rip the girls apart and tow them out alone, against their will, into the unknown.

Cold sucked at their bones, leaving them stiff and cramped. They were so fragile, yet the storm never lost any power. No one dared mention the lurking threat of sharks.

Perla was the first to die. She could no longer maintain her grip. As her strength ebbed, panic overcame her will to keep kicking. In horror, the girls watched as their delicate, wide-eyed childhood playmate slipped into eternity with an exhausted whimper. Timid Perla sank gracefully under the waves and was gone.

SULUAN

The shock of Perla's death screamed into the vacuum of their silence. Her cry wailed louder than the crash of waves around them. The bitter reality of death hit harder than the storm. Antonia immediately thought of Ofelia's brother, Jhun, who had captured Perla's attention, and she wondered if he was still alive.

Then her thoughts drifted to Carlo.

Did all the boys survive the storm? Where were they? Was her fisherman father on his way to find her before she was lost forever out at sea?

Doubts tormented her. Thirst overcame the girls, and they decided to try to drink a bit of seawater. It was terribly salty and caused most of them to vomit.

Days and nights passed with agony. For hours on end they simply floated together, barely clinging to both life and sanity as they battled every imaginable fear. But most of the time the friends drifted in silence. The girls saw no land -- just a vast sky and endless water.

The storm had somewhat subsided, but the currents stubbornly drove the girls to places in the sea they had never been before. Out beyond them were the uncharted waters of the great Pacific, the Philippine Deep Sea, as the fishermen called it.

In their frightened imaginations, it loomed ahead like a bottomless blue grave that waited to ingest them. The waves pulled them forward, tearing at them and dragging them away from their homeland.

Antonia worried.

Magellan and his crew certainly have been here before, and now we girls share a similar fate. We have no food and no fresh water to sustain our voyage -- our unintended voyage.

Daisy and Carlo's wedding day, and all the plans they had made, floated away from their thoughts like a wistful dream. Daisy was especially still and withdrawn. Antonia wiped her face free from a strand of seaweed and studied the faces of her dear friends round about her.

The sweet, somewhat-automatic smiles they habitually wore had disappeared. Etched on each young face now was pure horror. Love and pity rose simultaneously in her, and she ached for the words to bring comfort into their fear. But reassuring words played hide and seek in her mind, strangled by her own terror.

Intense heat gradually filled the morning of the next day. Sunshine unabashedly burst over the horizon with great force, driving away the leftover murkiness from the last week of stormy weather.

With this blast of light, it was as if the storm had never existed. The girls welcomed the sunshine into their dreary world because it brought warmth to thaw their chilled bodies.

The streams of sunlight chased away the hopelessness that had burrowed deep within them as the days passed. Clear yellow rays washed over them and melted a bit of the anxiety that had erupted the moment the sailboat capsized.

Perhaps in the light someone would see them. Some fishing boat would eventually pass by and discover the five bobbing. That was the cry of Antonia's heart. In this new light they could see farther. Searching for oncoming boats or far-away islands became the sole activity of the day.

As morning turned to high noon, however, these heavenly beams brought with them a fierce, scorching heat. The reflection of the sun danced on every ripple and sparkled like millions of dazzling diamonds, blinding the girls. With no shade tree, no palm leaves to cover their heads, the girls began to bake.

By the end of this day the sun had worn them out.

When it took its rest in the distant western sky, the girls' flesh was reddened, blistered, and sore to the touch. Once again, they each took miniscule sips of the salty water -- it was all they had. Once again, it caused them to vomit.

The night descended with a cool breeze, and the girls found sleep came easily. They took turns in the night watch; three of them dozed while two remained awake. The ocean rocked them, and currents carried them farther and farther out into nowhere.

It was now their tenth day at sea -- they knew this because they carved marks on the ship's mast with their fingernails. Daisy and Ofelia had been the pair on watch together through the night, and as the morning dawned, it was obvious that they had talked each other into a state of mutual panic.

Thoughts of a foreboding death at sea had tormented the girls' minds all night. The sun rose again, and both girls wept uncontrollably.

Ofelia found it difficult to breath. She rocked back and forth in the water and could not stay still. Daisy began to hallucinate; she saw ships that were not there and grabbed at invisible wedding presents on the water's surface.

She called out for Carlo and grew louder and more aggressive. Disoriented and confused, Daisy and Ofelia refused words of comfort from the girls, so Antonia and Lita came to their sides and held them tightly.

These were typical symptoms of dehydration and sunstroke, but the girls thought their friends were going crazy before their eyes. Perhaps they were.

The inescapable sun filled the long day. All day long, the young women endured throbbing headaches. Their joints ached, and their parched lips bled. Their once caramel-colored skin had burnt to a deep black.

Their beautiful flowing hair had stiffened in the salty air as the sunshine bleached the dark ink strands to a strange tint of pale orangey-rust brown.

At the end of the tenth day, Daisy and Ofelia passed away. The craziness began in the morning, intensified with the heat, and culminated in the early evening as the sun left its heavenly post for the night.

Perhaps it was the fear to face yet another night in pitch darkness that overcame their sanity. Perhaps it was weariness of the soul. Hopelessness drove them to the point of resignation.

After long hours floating together in the brackish, bottomless ocean, the day ended rudely when both despondent girls simultaneously let loose of the mast and sank quickly out of sight. The sudden death caught the remaining girls off guard. They froze in shock.

Lita and Bevs surrounded Antonia like bookends, just like in the cave at their last supper. They huddled tightly together in their grief and wept loudly into the empty night.

Three lonely girls were left, unable to find rest or solace in one another's company. Each clung desperately to the submerged mast and faced another hauntingly sinister night alone in the deep.

"Is anyone looking for us?" Bevs cried out into the darkness.

"They've given up," said Lita bitterly. "The storm was too long -- they must believe we've all drowned by now."

They were harsh words to hear, but perhaps they were true. Lita burned with fever, and the cooler night air brought her no relief, neither from the fever nor from the unrest that smoldered within her.

Bevs began to cry again. Her control gave way.

"We are going to die," she said.

Her chest hurt as she struggled with every breath.

"But they can't give up... we're still alive! We're still out here! Sharks could eat us alive! But oh, our fathers must be frantic looking for us," she said, this time with greater sadness and pity in her voice.

Hunger pangs had besieged Bev's stomach for several days. She knew that her friends also starved, and yet no one shared her pain openly.

Carlo will come for us. Antonia began to dream and squinted up at the sun.

She thought of Carlo's strength of spirit -- of Papa Beni's tender ways and of Mam Salud and her hearty laughter. They had raised their grandson to be a fine man. Then she remembered Daisy. *Daisy was gone. Ofelia was gone. Perla was gone.*

Waking nightmares robbed Antonia of the peace she was desperate to keep. She loved her cousin Lita despite her bossiness. She adored her life-long friend, Bevs. They only had one another now.

They were too young to die abandoned at sea like pirates or Magellan's sailors. Her mind drifted and became blank. The steady ripples of water hit her with a hypnotic rhythm.

Ok, Ok, Ok... Antonia tried to encourage herself. Her mind spun. *Love will find me out here. Love makes me unafraid. Come on, Tonya -- remember your family. Think about little Rosalyn, about home, about school next year. Just concentrate. Think of something. The cave. The cliffs. Suluan.*

It was hard to focus. She chanted the words of her hope like a prayer to calm her unsettled heart. The waves lifted and dropped her again and again and again. Soon the chant died out into a sporadic mutter of garbled words that made no sense.

Tonight the infinite sky overflowed with twinkling stars, as if someone had poked pinholes through a heavy blanket to allow miniscule fragments of light to shine through to her side. Now the beautiful array of stars offered Antonia no joy or marvel, as they had in the past. She simply passed time tonight, wondering what to do when daylight came.

One prayer for each star she counted. Hope hid deep behind the darkness of the night. Somewhere behind that black sky was light. This thought overwhelmed her mind, and once again she felt small and insignificant floating alone at sea.

Antonia began quietly humming an old song from her childhood to still her fears. Then she remembered the soft hands of her mother the day she had left for the wedding.

What were those last words she spoke to me?

Her thoughts trailed off as she examined the patterns in the myriad of pinholes above her. She realized that her mind was losing its ability to focus.

In the early hours of the eleventh day, Antonia startled and awoke after she drifted off to sleep. Someone had to stay awake. All three had struggled desperately through most of the night against fatigue in an attempt to keep watch over the other two.

As she opened her eyes and tried to focus, she noticed that her vision was blurry and dim. Bevs squatted on the half-sunken ship. She leaned forward against the mast in water that came above her hunched shoulders. Bevs was still asleep. Antonia looked over her shoulder, but she did not see Lita.

"Lit!" she cried. "Where are you, Lita?"

No answer. Lita was nowhere in sight.

Bevs jerked her head up when she heard Antonia's cry. They both desperately searched the waters, but Lita was gone. Bevs hung her expressionless face and let out a long pitiful moan. The girls were too sad and tired to cry. Neither of them spoke a word.

They positioned themselves again around the ever-sturdy wooden mast, entwined their arms at the elbows, and weakly leaned their wet backs against each other for support. Once again, they searched the sea around them, yearning for some sign of life, terrified of the sight of shark fins. Exhaustion left them drained and empty.

The sun belligerently paraded itself high in the cloudless, azure sky. This vicious cycle of pain came again to taunt them with its maddening heat. Sunshine was supposed to be a cheery friend, but no longer was it welcome in their world.

Noon now subjugated sea and sky. They hated the hot sun all day and sought relief as they splashed the salty water over their heads to keep themselves cool as the hours passed.

Sky and sea. Air and water. Clouds and waves. A monotone, monotonous canvas: blue on blue as far as the eye could see.

The two best friends clung to each other and rarely spoke. Talking became difficult as their lips and tongues swelled, cracked, and bled. Their shriveled skin reminded them that they were slowly dying. They didn't want to know it, didn't want to face it, but death demanded entrance.

Another day to mark off with a scratch on the wooden mast -- there was again no sign of help. This was the eleventh day at sea. Long red streaks of color shot dramatically across the sky in the late afternoon.

The girls lay their heavy heads on their folded arms wrapped together around the mast. Their sun-bleached hair floated in many directions like wild seaweed on the surface of the water.

Faces bloated with expressionless features, their bodies

wasted away without food or water, Antonia and Bevs continued to drift aimlessly. In her heart, Antonia begged God for food.

"Anything," she pleaded softly, "just something to fill the gnawing hunger inside of me."

Bevs lifted her head instinctively to look one last time for some sign of help before the sun completely set. She let out a gasp and called to Antonia, who slowly rose and strained to see where Bevs pointed.

"Look, Tonya... over there!" said Bevs with a cracked voice. "It's a faint island. It is right over there; do you see it?"

"I want to see it, Bevs... but I can't see clearly. My eyes are funny, and it's hard to figure out if that is an island or just a cloud. Oh, I hope it's land!"

"It is! It is! We're close enough to be seen by fishermen who sail out this way."

Bevs spoke with new strength in her voice, and a slight smile returned to her otherwise sullen face. The girls went with thoughts of rescue into the night hours. They scanned the distance for lights with eyes wide open. Tomorrow they would need strength to kick toward this mysterious isle.

But sleep would not come to Antonia. Her thoughts traveled back to her own island, her beloved village where her feet could touch the ground. There, she knew every hut, every child, and every wooden boat along the shoreline.

Thoughts of their last venture up to the cave brought her comfort as night fell.

CHAPTER ELEVEN
THE JOURNEY

Disconnected. Drifting. Detached. She was just like Suluan. Those were Antonia's first thoughts as she woke on the twelfth day. The island girl lost at sea without a lighthouse to attract attention, without a cave to hide in to escape from the storm and the sun.

Out alone at sea, dangers lurked in deep, dark places she could not see. There was nothing to stand on. There was no solid ground under her weary legs.

Bevs, her dearest friend in the world, lay motionless, face down beside her.

Antonia closed her eyes, held her breath, and shook Bevs in a hope against hope that what she feared had not happened. No response came from Bevs. Antonia grabbed her friend and shook her harder and harder. Her head began to spin, and her heart beat wildly.

Antonia released her pent-up breath with a long, agonized sigh. She reached out and pulled the dead body of Bevs to herself and cradled her in her weak arms. She rocked back and forth in shock and disbelief.

As the two floated together, Antonia thought of all she had lost in the last few days. Family. Home. Friends. And now Bevs -- she was more than a friend, more than a sister. A volcano of pain brooded under the surface of her soul.

From deep within Antonia came a painful wail of grief

that shook her to her core. The intensity of her loss overwhelmed her. Her cries turned to hysteria. She screamed into the gentle breeze that innocently blew over the waters.

Antonia hated the skies that had stolen her innocence, her simplicity, and her sheltered life -- and now her best friend. She hated being left alone. Antonia lifted her face to accuse the heavens and opened her mouth wide, but not a word came out.

Of course, this was not God's fault; she knew better than to waste her failing voice on any sort of blame toward Him. She also knew that He heard the prayer of her heart even louder than the murmured words on her painful lips.

Antonia lifted Bevs' limply-hanging head to her own. She smothered Bevs' face with painful kisses. She stared intently at her, trying to capture her features in her mind, and vowed never to forget her bosom friend who had been born with her on Suluan.

In a faint whisper she said to Bevs, "Good bye, my darling little sister."

An hour passed. The time came to push Bevs out to sea.

"I... will... miss... you."

She watched the silvery waves carry Bevs away until she could see her no more.

All alone, she floated in silence. Hours passed.

This journey is now my own. Here I am at the mercy of a big God, with His big blue world of sea and sky. I am small and insignificant -- just like I've always felt. But now, I am really, truly alone. All alone.

She floated motionless for hours, unable to think straight, unable to grasp her complete desolation. Sadness absorbed Antonia into a pitiful place of misery. Loneliness was like a fever, hot within her now. Her eyes grew dim, and the pain in her chest and abdomen increased every time she inhaled.

The saltwater lapped incessantly all around her as the sun beat down upon her from every angle. She was a prisoner of the giant sea. Her eyes closed. Sun streams burnt Antonia's face as the wind whispered Carlo's name. She floated on top of her sunken wedding ship.

I'm still alive. My head is throbbing. I can hear my breath. I can hear my heart beat. Remind me why I live and breathe.

The faint shadow of what might be an island was no longer of interest to Antonia. The water was a dull silver-gray like a dreary shroud that closed in on her from every side. Her spirits were at their lowest, and now she battled depression as violently as she had battled the storm.

Uncertainty and doubt tormented her. She lacked the will power to try to kick her way towards this so-called island.

What if it is just another hallucination?

When she did try to open her swollen eyes, her vision blurred. She could no longer trust her senses, so she just hung to her faithful mast and passively floated all morning as the reddish ball rolled its way again up into the middle of the hot field of sky.

When she tried once again to open her eyes later on in the day, she saw a long piece of wood about two yards away. On it was half a coconut and three cooked bananas; God had heard her prayer! She stretched out her hand to snatch the food. She was starving to death.

However, the cramps and pain in her stomach spoke and reminded her that if she were to eat, she would have terrible indigestion and probably die. So with a kick of her leg, she pushed the board away.

"Thank you," she said with tears in her eyes.

A few minutes later, she realized what she had done.

Am I crazy? What did I do? I pushed away food!

She wrestled with her own thoughts as they spun out of control inside her head. Then she ripped off small pieces of her clothing and began to gnaw on them. The salt brine stung as her cracked lips touched the cloth.

Antonia wet her lips and throat with the seawater slowly, but she dared not swallow the water. It did not begin to quench her thirst, for her stomach began to cramp, and she started to vomit once again.

Antonia focused as often as she could on the shadowy form far away, which started to look more and more to her like an island. But she dared not hope, not yet. The sweltering day stretched out before her with no end.

Dying at sea would have been bad enough; dying alone at sea was unspeakable.

All my earthly treasures are buried at sea.

There was no help in sight. She lapsed in and out of consciousness all day.

As her head throbbed, she prayed, *Please, God, let this day pass quickly.*

Antonia tried to focus as she bobbed up and down. From deep within her, faith in the unseen Creator began to grow. She could feel it. She rolled over onto her back and stretched out her body to float effortlessly next to the ship.

She stared up to the filmy clouds above her and began to sing softly. "You give me hope in trouble. You give me peace when oceans are around. Lord, You calm me down. You are my light in darkness. Show me the way when I don't see the ground. Lord, you calm me down."

The wind picked up, and with it, small waves with their whitecaps danced all around her. Towards late afternoon something else, this time much larger, floated in her direction. It was the body of Bevs.

At first it was hard to figure out who it was, as Bevs was face down in the water with her tangled hair streaming chaotically around her head on the water's surface.

Without a second thought, Antonia grabbed a fistful of Bev's hair and struggled to pull the body up onto the sunken sailboat. Uncontrollably, Antonia shivered. Her best friend had returned to her.

As she had done throughout their young lives, Antonia slowly braided Bevs' long mass of knotted hair, but this time she wove it onto the mast to secure her friend to the boat. Left over middle, right over middle, left over middle -- carefully, lovingly, gradually lacing the locks in and out of one another, the way she had always taken care of her friend.

Antonia meticulously picked strands of seaweed out of Bevs' hair until it was clean. Now she had company for the long night ahead. She and Bevs would spend the night together; her bosom friend, the keeper of her childhood secrets, was with her again.

As darkness encompassed the daylight, her friend grew suddenly strange to her, for Bevs' body began to glow. The eerie, phosphorous light that her body emitted from head to toe frightened Antonia. She closed her eyes tightly and fought off the urge to scream or cry. Eventually she settled her heart and found peace.

Bevs was now her light in the darkness. Antonia told Bevs her memories of their childhood, their dreams and secrets, and how dear Bevs had been to her. She could still think straight as long as long as she talked to her friend.

"God," she spoke in a tiny voice to the great heavens above, "please come into this chaos. Come into my despair. Please, please bring me Your help. Save me." She waited for a response. Nothing. Her heart beat loudly, but she still felt a strange peace.

The expanse of the cosmos filled with miniature lights

stretched as far as she could see. The sight overwhelmed her once again. She tried to focus beyond the depth of the cavernous canopy over her, and as she did, the eternal sense of never-ending-ness made her frail body shiver with reverence and awe.

A falling star grabbed center stage high above Antonia's head. Like a sign from her Creator, Antonia took this wild stroke of light as a message from God underscoring His greatness before her eyes.

"God of the universe. God of these heavens. God of all creation. God of the impossible. God of the deep sea where I cannot touch bottom. I know You see me down here in Your ocean. My every need. My little strength. I give it to You. You are more than enough for me. Please rescue me. I feel too young to travel this far from home."

With these reverential pleas and a tiny spark of hope, Antonia somberly watched through the starlit night and waited. She repeated her song in the night.

"You give me peace when oceans are around. Lord, You calm me down. You are my light in darkness. Show me the way when I don't see the ground. Whatever was, whatever is, whatever will be -- I need You every day."

The morning of the thirteenth day arrived. Today Antonia had a much clearer view of what Bevs had pointed out to her before she died. Despite her faded vision, she had seen what looked like an invitation: a beautiful island with trees and a rocky shoreline.

It was still too far away for her to tell whether the land was inhabited, but to Antonia it looked like paradise -- and almost like Suluan. Surely, if people live there, they will be out fishing in these waters.

All day Antonia searched the sea for boats, for any sign of life. Late in the afternoon, as the expansive awning above her took on its evening glow and the sun loomed low on the faraway horizon, she heard a whooshing sound around her.

A shark fin and part of its body surfaced at a high rate of speed before it disappeared into the water again. The waters around the boat churned with large, savage shadows. Antonia gasped.

Chills of terror gripped her when she saw a pack of sharks, some half as long as the sunken sailboat. They circled around and around the two girls. The agitated waters splashed up around her on all sides.

All her life, she had heard of these predators of the deep. Gruesome stories fishermen told during mealtimes had haunted her as a young girl. One particular gory tale of a basketball player from Guiuan came instantly to Antonia's mind.

On his way to the island of Homonhon, his boat had capsized, and a shark devoured him. Three days later a fisherman caught this same shark and was shocked to discover the poor boy's basketball uniform and a remnant of his body in the stomach of the shark. His remains were buried back home on Guiuan in a simple grave.

Frantically, she reached for the mast and tried as best she could to shimmy up the unstable wooden pole to escape them. Antonia's head throbbed, and she felt nauseous again.

Then it hit her.

They must be in a feeding frenzy because of Bevs. That's why they've come. They can smell her!

Her hands shook with fear, but Antonia yanked free the tangled braid attached to the pole, and with her foot pushed her darling Bevs quickly away from the ship. She had turned her most cherished friend into bait for hungry sea-monsters.

No sooner had the body of Bevs left the mast than the

biggest of the sharks furiously attacked. It snapped the body in two with its massive jaws. Her small body jerked unnaturally from side to side in the middle of the thrashing swarm.

Then the other sharks had a feast; they mauled the corpse until nothing was left. Antonia shrieked in horror and cupped her hand over her mouth. She would be next.

The school of sinister, pointy-nosed sharks continued to encircle the boat, their massive bodies so close she could reach down and touch their plastic-looking skin. Bevs had not been enough to satisfy them.

Antonia hung helpless and weak to a lone rope still attached to the mast and desperately tried to lift herself high above the reddened waters -- and suddenly, a much larger shark appeared.

More than twice as long as the sailboat -- she guessed about forty feet. It was the largest shark she had ever seen in her life! The water around the boat became eerily still. He had chased her predators away.

What kind of a shark is this? They must all be afraid of him. Look at the size of his head...his back fin...his tail is so wide!

The gargantuan fish circled slowly back and forth and cut through the glass-like crimson surface with its enormous fin. It circled leisurely around Antonia's dangling feet. His flattened head sported a blunt snout above its enormously wide mouth.

She could see through the water that it had short barbells protruding from its nostrils. His back and sides were more brown than gray, and his back was like a checkerboard, spotted white among pale vertical and horizontal stripes. His two large dorsal fins were set rearward on his long, torpedo body.

This monster of all monsters calmly whirled around Antonia for several minutes, and then he did something very unusual for a shark. He halted at the pole, exactly under Antonia, and peacefully stayed for a few minutes. She froze in terror and held her breath, expecting the shark to bite into her side.

Then, just as quickly as he had appeared, he turned his broad tail and swam away into the deep. Her heart raced as she watched him leave. Of course, she had heard of these great creatures of the sea, but had never imagined that she would be so close to one. What was even stranger was when he later returned.

She clung to the dangling rope and the crooked wooden mast. Her arms and legs had grown weak as the evening wore on. Despite her weariness, she did not intend to return to the water to float for fear of the sharks' return.

The sun had long since settled and the night had arrived when Antonia saw out in the distance a long row of miniature lights, like a string of flickering candles upon the water's surface.

How strange. Perhaps it's the huge shark. Maybe I am dreaming -- or worse, maybe I am seeing things and going crazy!

Then all at once, the mammoth shark rose up underneath her. Antonia screamed. This creature of the deep, in all his leathery greatness, appeared without a sound. He stopped swimming, simply hovered over the submerged boat, and then slowly pushed the boat and Antonia's frail body down under the water again.

The shark gradually moved up to the surface, close to Antonia, and rubbed his silvery polka-dotted skin against her body. Confused and choked with fear, she could not figure out what the shark wanted. He returned four times. Each time he rubbed up against her legs under the water.

Repeatedly, the shark seemed to invite her; he courted her to ride. His lower pectoral fin embraced her body intimately, making it easy for Antonia to straddle the shark's back.

She held her breath and slowly released the wooden mast from her panicked grip. Antonia hesitated a moment and then sank onto the smooth vinyl back of this new sea friend. With a leg on each side of the shark, Antonia grabbed his dorsal fin, took a deep breath, and closed her eyes.

Is this a dream?

She shook with unbelief as she thought of what she had just done. The light weight of her young, emaciated body was barely aboard the shark as he gently moved forward. As if to see that Antonia was secure and safe, the great fish paused.

He kept his spotted body close to the surface and made sure that he did not lose his passenger as he cut through the water. She did not know whether to laugh, cry, or scream for joy -- or for fear.

The gigantic shark swam toward the unknown island in the dark hours of late evening. He traveled forty minutes or more, as if he knew instinctively where to take his frightened passenger. Antonia's spindle thin legs dragged lifelessly through the dark rippled wake on either side of the mammoth fish.

For most of the trip, she had kept her eyes closed. She was afraid to look and often held her breath, praying fervently.

This has to be a miracle. My miracle!

Although the trip provided excitement, the truth was that she was weak and close to death. As the shark began to slow down, Antonia gradually stretched her stiffened legs to search for sturdy footing on the sandy floor beneath her.

Wobbly and unsteadily, she cautiously dismounted her steed and stumbled backward in an attempt to keep as far as possible from his oversized mouth, which was much, much longer than the width of a grown man's outstretched arms.

What a mouth he has! As if this was a big smile for me!
Antonia had to laugh to herself.
As long as he's not hungry tonight, I guess I'm safe.

CHAPTER TWELVE
THE ARRIVAL

Antonia turned her back to the great fish to find the shore, she heard a splash behind her. She turned around and saw that her rescuer had returned to the deep sea. He headed in the direction of her capsized boat.

"Farewell, Ihutiki," she called after him in a raspy voice as she feebly blew a kiss into the night air.

Antonia fumbled painstakingly through the thigh-high water. Even the smallest of waves that splashed around her made her fall. She had no strength to stand and barely the will to make it to the darkened beach just twenty feet in front of her. She felt her way to a big jagged rock along the shoreline.

Although she did not know it at the time, she had landed on the island of Dinagat approximately 55 miles southwest of Suluan. Dinagat Island was known as one of the holiest sites among the islands of the Philippines during the pre-Christian era.

A native legend held that the god of hurricanes was persuaded to surrender his attacks on the islands because of "Da", the god of peace.

Antonia crawled up as high as she could on this sun-warmed boulder and curled up into a tight ball. She was exhausted, but the strangeness of this new place and the crazy memory of her shark ride, kept sleep far from her.

Every muscle in her small frame ached; her head

pounded with pain, and her burned skin rubbed raw against the rough stone. However, she was no longer moving... no longer floating, no longer drifting, and no longer bobbing in the bottomless Pacific.

The rock beneath her still held the heat from the day and stood solid and stable. This was something Antonia had not felt for almost two weeks as she wandered at sea like a nomad. But she felt like she was still moving.

Antonia finally succumbed to sleep under the starry sky with faded thoughts of home and of friends now lost. Deep in slumber, she never saw the shooting stars that danced above her all night long.

In the faint light of the next day, Antonia began to stir. The soreness in her chest, stomach and head informed her that she was still alive. The last weeks had been like a bad dream. She shivered, barely clothed in her ripped dress.

She could not open her engorged eyes. The salt had dried like glue, and her lashes and the rims of her eyelids were stuck together. Her eyes burned beneath her lids. Her breathing was slow and shallow. She lay still, and listened to the sounds around her, unable to lift her head or move.

Gentle waves washed upon the shore. The leaves of nearby palm trees rustled as the wind blew over her skeletal form.

She heard no voices, but she could make out a few crow calls from far away roosters. These were the familiar sounds of island life, but Antonia knew she was not in Suluan. She could also tell by the coolness of the air that the morning sun had not yet risen.

An hour or two passed when at last a lone fishing boat passed by close to the right of her rock. A single elderly man, who had been out fishing the whole night, glanced up to the spot where Antonia lay, still curled tightly in a ball. She looked a frightful sight to him, as if she had washed ashore and been abandoned on the beach for months.

Fearing that he had stumbled upon a dead body, he ran without a word to find help.

The old man returned quickly, curious but full of apprehension, with two of his friends. They stood far off and called to her.

"Kinsa ka? Who are you?"

Antonia heard their voices, muffled in her head, but she was unable to rise, unable to respond or utter even a sound. Fear gripped her.

Again, they called and asked her name.

"Taga dis-a ka? From where are you?"

No answer. She did not understand this strange dialect.

Hesitantly, the men came closer to Antonia and quietly climbed up the side of the rock to get a better view. They saw her emaciated condition up close as they crouched over her. They shook their heads sadly and clucked their tongues as a sign of resignation.

Very carefully, the older man bent over to lift her up into his arms, unsure if she was still breathing or not. The men decided to carry her into their fishing boat and row to the larger neighboring village, Quezon, to find help.

In the small fishing boat, the men could not keep their eyes off Antonia; shocked and saddened by her deathly condition, they rowed as fast as they could around the tip of the island as the sun peeked lazily, with its far-reaching rays, into the new day. The oldest fisherman reached out and stroked Antonia's disheveled, sun-scorched hair as if she were his own daughter. He removed his lightweight jacket and to carefully cover her frailty.

Her long hair was now thick and stiff with salt, her puffed-up eyes swollen shut, her skin burnt black and wrinkled beyond description, in many places blistered and open. She was no longer conscious. She heard neither the dip and splash of the oars nor the whispers of the worried old men.

Their wrinkled brows deepened with concern for the unknown girl from the sea. The oldest man wagged his head in dismay and bowed to speak a prayer over her lifeless form. His eye caught sight of the twisted shark tooth necklace around her neck.

"I wonder where she is from," he said softly. "I have never seen this child around here." The old man held his hand over his mouth and shook his head in disbelief.

"Should we try to give the poor girl some water?"

"No! We dare not. If she dies, they will all think it was because of us. Let's just get to shore and find help as quickly as we can!"

After they landed, the men left Antonia alone in the boat and took off in a sprint to locate the barangay captain of the village.

Agatha Sayson walked along the shoreline in Quezon. She had her well-worn woven basket slung over her shoulder as she meandered barefoot up and down the water's edge, searching for crabs and seaweed in the early hours of the day.

She enjoyed the quiet and coolness of this new dawn and was in no hurry to return home, where her family was undoubtedly busy with breakfast preparations and household chores. Agatha was more than content to stroll along the beach and let her mind wander out across the ocean and up into the pale blue sky.

Tiny crabs scurried underfoot along the entire

coastline, running out of one hole in the sand into another. They made the ground dance with activity. Their playful antics never ceased to entertain Agatha.

In the last hour, she had adeptly captured her fair share of crabs that she planned to cook for today's lunch. They were still active, and they tried to escape out of her covered basket.

Ok. I'm done. Time to get back home.

She had not grown up here in the village of Quezon on Dinagat Island, but came from a much larger place -- the town of Anahawan in Southern Leyte. Narciso Sayson, her handsome husband of almost twenty-four years, had married her when she was still a young teenage girl, and they had settled here in his birthplace.

Despite the happy years they had lived in Quezon, Agatha always battled home-sickness and longed for her family, who lived north of here on the island of Leyte. Memories of her younger years on Leyte held her heart captive with their far-reaching tentacles.

She never really wanted to be here, but she was, and she was making the best of it. That was what Agatha did best.

She was in her late thirties, but she looked younger. Her four-foot frame was still slim and energetic, crowned with enviably long black hair parted down the middle, and despite her nostalgia for home she always wore a cheerful demeanor.

She had raised four children; her son Pedro was already twenty-three, while Peping, Solidad, and Quirino were teens. Agatha was a loving mother, an immaculate housekeeper, and a good cook.

Agatha hummed softly to herself as she passed a group of small fishing boats tied up to tree stumps and rocks along the edge of the water. She heard a faint groan from within one of the old boats. A moment later came a bump -- and then another groan.

She scanned the row of boats and there, covered with a tattered navy-blue jacket and wedged between fishing rods, a sharp harpoon, and fishing nets, lay a crumpled girl. The poor sea-maiden held her head between cracked hands, and her mouth was open slightly, as if she had just tried to speak. Agatha could not imagine why she was asleep in the boat or why she looked so battered.

Agatha dropped her basket and clamored down into the boat. She crouched beside the girl and tenderly lifted her head into her lap. Her silky head bent gently over the skeleton-frame of a teenage girl.

"Day," she spoke into her ear, "Kinsa ka? Who are you?"

No answer.

Again, she tried, "Day, taga di a ka? Where are you from?"

No response.

Then Antonia spoke. She struggled to move her swollen tongue, and the word came out painfully.

"Loto," she said slowly.

Strange. Loto? What kind of dialect is that? Agatha wondered. Then she repeated her question, "Kinsa ka, day? Who are you, my child? Why are you here in this boat?"

"Loto," repeated Antonia, this time a bit louder in a cracked voice.

"Well, I don't know what you are trying to tell me, but I see that you are not well. So if it is okay with you, you are coming home with me, little one," Agatha said in a calm tone.

Agatha lifted Antonia's meager frame up into her sinewy brown arms, tucked in the old blue jacket around her mid-section, and carried her onto the shore. She left her basket of crabs behind and headed home with her new charge. The feather-light girl lay limp in her arms.

Her husband, Narciso, would be home soon. He had left before dawn to go fishing.

Funny.

Agatha laughed to herself.

His last words to me this morning were, 'Maybe I will catch a mermaid today.' Wait until he sees what I brought home!

CHAPTER THIRTEEN
THE WELCOME

The nipa-thatched home was set back ten yards from the main road. Its clean-swept yard, neatly bordered by a fence, boasted a plentiful array of tropical plants. Banana and papaya trees lined one side of the yard, and Filipino orange trees grew tall around the border of the other. The trees shaded the entire garden area.

Chickens and ducks scurried among the tree trunks. The house stood about six feet above the ground, and in the cool under the home, a fat pinkish pig tied to a long dusty tether grunted and squealed all day long.

As Agatha entered the front door, she smelled the pungent aroma of fried buwad, dried salted fish. Strong June sunlight poured through each window. She stood in the center of the sala, the living room, not knowing what to do first.

Her arms quivered, and her forehead dampened with nervous perspiration. She feared this young girl was near to death -- or had just died in her arms on her way home.

From outside came a mocking call from a bird that laughed at her attempt to help this unknown person. From the back of the house, she could hear the clatter of pots and the chatter among her children as they washed their clothes and prepared breakfast over the open fire outside in their "dirty kitchen," where they could fry foods without filling the house with smoke.

Agatha panicked. Her eyes darted around the room.

What should I do now? What should I do with the girl?
"What if…" she said aloud, "What if she is already dead?"

Narciso came smiling through the front door, a string full of freshly caught Bangus fish in his clenched hand. He was glad to be home after a long morning out on the sea. Narciso was a good man, a strong provider, as kind and gregarious as his sons after him. He froze when he saw the withered body in his wife's arms.

He ran to find a stack of blankets in their bedroom and then laid them over the long bamboo-slatted bench to create a cushion. After fumbling the blankets smooth, he returned to help Agatha carry the girl over to the corner of the room to lay her down.

"Sus, Maria, Joseph…! What in heaven's name have you brought home with you, my dear? This is *some* catch!" he stammered in a half-whisper.

"Aw, dad, you won't believe it when I tell you. I found the poor thing alone in a fishing boat just now," explained Agatha. "She is barely breathing, and she looks like she has roasted out in the sun forever. I have no idea where she's from or who she is, and…" her voice trailed off into silence.

She choked back tears and swallowed hard.

"Wasn't anyone around the boat, my dear? Did she talk to you?" said Narciso.

"All she said was 'Loto' -- but I have no idea what she meant," said Agatha. "She looks like she is… dying. And, well, what should we, uh… *do* with her? I didn't have the heart to leave her alone in that old fishing boat."

Narciso's voice went quiet. He stared down at his dark, leathery hands. He smelled of fish and the sea.

He thought for a moment and said, "I think it would

be best if I got Nanding Navarro. He needs to know what is going on, just in case. As barangay captain, he will know if anyone from another village has been reported missing."

Agatha lifted her eyebrows in agreement and pointed with her lips toward the door.

"Please hurry," she said.

She ran to the bedroom and found a lightweight cloth to cover Antonia's half-nakedness.

Narciso left, and Agatha disappeared for a moment to find her children and some fresh water for the girl. Three of the four children were home, and when they saw the worried look on their mother's face, they dropped their work and gathered around her.

"Ma... what is wrong?" asked Peping. "You look like you have seen a Wok-Wok! Did something bad happen? Is it Pedro? Is it Daddy?"

"*Pssst!* Come quickly," said Agatha as she motioned with her flying hand signal and returned to the living area.

She dipped down into the water bucket and filled a cup on her way out of the kitchen area. Peping, Solidad, and Quirino followed close on her heels. Solidad, the Saysons' only girl, looked about the same age as Antonia. She knelt down at her side and gave her mother a somber glance.

Agatha whispered the whole story quickly. Peping and Quirino came close to examine Antonia's gnarled hands, thin feet, and blistered face. They lingered in silence, holding their breath as they strained to hear hers.

"We should let her rest, and we will just wait until Papa returns with news from Mr. Navarro. This girl is near death, and we don't want to do anything to harm her," said Agatha softly as she sat cross-legged next to Solidad and put her hand on Antonia's forehead.

"Ma," asked Peping hesitantly, "shouldn't we at least

try to give the girl something to drink or to eat?"

"Yes, you're right. I've got a bit of water here to drop onto her lips, but I think it's best that we let her sleep and not wake her," responded Agatha. "It feels as if she has a high fever, and I am worried that she was in the sun too long. Just look at her poor face. She is so pitiful."

The four said nothing for several minutes watching their patient -- the dying girl from the seashore. Then Solidad drew a deep breath and turned to face her mother.

"If," she said, "if she lives and wants to stay with us, can we keep her, Ma?"

Agatha stood up and looked over her shoulder at her boys with a grin. They all stifled the urge to laugh at Solidad's adolescent request.

"I'm afraid we have to simply leave this in the Lord's hands," said Agatha as she helped her daughter stand to her feet and pulled her into an embrace.

"We will take one day at a time and do our best to help this little mermaid recover. Heaven only knows where her parents are and how worried they must be. I can barely imagine their grief."

"We'll be her new family," said Quirino. "That is, of course, if she needs one."

Peping nodded silently.

Agatha began to drop bits of water from her fingertips into the slightly-open mouth of Antonia. Solidad squatted on the floor next to the bed and watched her mother as the strange girl slept. The boys tiptoed out and returned to their chores with heads and hearts full of unanswered questions.

Agatha gave the cup of water to her daughter and ran next door to her younger sister's house, knowing that Pilar would want to know all the details of what was going on this morning.

Pilar, the chatterbox in the family, was talking with a group of village women who had stopped in front of her small home on their way back from buying fresh fish and vegetables at the morning market. This was routine for them.

Well-worn paths led from all directions of town directly to the prim white-picket fence that framed her postage-stamp sized plot of land and three-room nipa house. Pilar was opinionated and capable enough to manage not only her own concerns but also the woes of others.

Women of all ages made it a point to stop by Pilar's house to fill her in on all of their personal comings and goings. It was, in some odd way, their daily duty. She was a professional listener.

She did not see herself as a gossip -- but rather as a gatherer of essential information, much like the local newspaper or daily radio broadcasts from Manila.

She had never held back information about anything in her whole life, and so she had gained her reputation in Quezon. She operated both the geographical and the social center of the town with a cheerful, non-judgmental heart.

Even though Pilar was Agatha's younger sister, she looked out for her older sister and her sister's four children. Pilar was the only member of Agatha's family who lived close-by, so Agatha treasured her motherly care.

"*Pssst!* Pilar! Excuse me, huh..." called Agatha as she waved to the group of women. "Sorry to interrupt, but I must speak with you! Karon. Now."

Pilar said her good-byes, seeing her sister's urgency, and hurried to join Agatha, who sat on a small-slated wooden bench outside of Pilar's front door. Agatha shifted her weight back and forth.

She rocked a bit nervously and swung her feet in small circles over the dusty ground. Subconsciously, she bit her lip and squeezed her eyes tightly shut in an attempt to figure out what to do next.

Pilar knew something was amiss.

She sat down next to Agatha, tucked in her floral print dress tightly under her legs, and smoothed down her fly-away hair, as if to prepare herself for what Agatha was about to share with her. She was a summer-skinned, petite woman with very white teeth and a big smile that she used often.

She reached out gingerly and tapped her sister on her shoulder to let her know she was there. Agatha sat up straight, took a deep breath, and gave Pilar a tearful, wide-eyed stare.

Agatha told Pilar all about the half-dead teenage girl she had found, the fishing boat, Mr. Navarro, and even Solidad's amusing question. When she was finally finished explaining everything in vivid detail, Pilar sprang to her feet impulsively and offered to run to find the village hilot, the natural healer who knew the medicinal benefit of every plant, root, and blossom on Dinagat Island.

"The *hilot*! If I go now, I can fetch him in ten minutes' time. Sir Salazar will definitely know what to give her," said Pilar with confidence.

"Oo. Yes, Pilar. That's a wonderful plan. But please just wait until Narciso returns. Maybe we will find the island nurse and have her take a look at the girl. In the meantime, I think I had better get home. You come over later today, okay? Salamat, day. Thank you, little sister. Sigi, lang. Bye-bye."

The two hugged, and Agatha headed home. Ten minutes later, Narciso arrived in the front yard with a small entourage of fishermen and the barangay captain, Nanding Navarro, all come to take a closer look at the strange girl who had been found on a rock that morning.

The three men who had brought her to Quezon trailed behind the group. They had returned to their fishing boat with the village officials only to find that the young girl had vanished. They had roamed up and down the shore to look for signs of her, but all they found was Agatha's basket of crabs until Narciso came and led them to his house.

Mr. Navarro gasped and put his hand to his mouth. He stood over the makeshift bed in the living room and took a hard look at Antonia to see if he recognized her. He squint his eyes and rubbed his bald head slowly.

He wore a pressed red plaid shirt whose sleeves had been rolled up past his elbows, a pair of freshly-washed khaki trousers, and brown sandals. But despite his neat clothing, his face looked as though he had just been dragged out of bed.

"Hmmmm... dili maayo. This does *not* look good," said the barangay captain under his breath. He surveyed the family members suspiciously.

Agatha's lips twitched. She felt guilty about what could be construed as interference with the island authorities. She hid her hands behind her back and wrung them restlessly.

"This young girl is barely breathing, and, quite honestly, it looks like she will die. We have no information about her and have no idea where she is from," he said.

Everyone stood silently and stared.

"By the way, Ma'am Sayson, were *you* the one who took her out of Eduardo's fishing boat this morning? Or was it one of your children here?"

Agatha stood close to Narciso and shyly answered, "Oo... Yes, Mr. Navarro, I am afraid it was me. I -- I just could not help myself. The poor girl was there in the boat, and no one was around, so I took her home with me." *He must think I broke the law.*

"Ma'am Sayson, never mind... trying to help a drowned girl is not against the law," he said. "I told these three men the same thing earlier this morning when they tried to find her. Are you and Narciso ready to assume full responsibility for her?"

He lowered his voice to a faint whisper and continued, "We don't know what to do with her, and I think she's too fragile to bring to the hospital in Cebu City. And," he paused and cleared his throat, "I *don't* believe she will live until tomorrow. Like I said, I think she's close to death."

"Sir, our family will try our best to help her," said Narciso. "She has a home with us now, and we will try to get her through the night. We won't leave her alone for a minute. Who knows -- maybe there is some reason that she landed by us like she did, some sacred design behind it all."

Mr. Navarro lifted his eyebrows and cocked his head. A smirk spread across his unshaven face. Then he shook Narciso's hand and wished him good luck with the girl with a few clucks of his tongue.

"Please let me know what happens," the mayor said as he turned to leave.

All the men took one long last look at Antonia, half-way hidden under the bed sheet. They turned to leave and thanked Agatha for her kindness. She watched as they walked a slow procession up the street.

How difficult it was to hear the barangay captain's negative assessment of Antonia. His words hit them all hard, like some final judgment of doom against their frail mermaid from who-knows-where. Agatha could feel her heart sink; affection for this unknown girl had already taken root in her soul.

No. We will not lose her.

She clutched her fist tightly and shuffled her bare feet back and forth on the wooden floor.

Later that morning, as all three children kept vigil around Antonia's bedside, Agatha slipped away to get some fresh air and to think. She walked out again to the shoreline behind their house. She found her basket filled with small crabs just where she had dropped it when she discovered Antonia.

Although the sun beat down unmercifully upon her, she lingered longer and walked pensively up and down the water's edge with the basket slung again over her shoulder.

Why me? Why our family? What could all of this mean? There must be some special purpose when extraordinary things like this happen. It's not every day that a total stranger washes up on the shore. Why did this girl come to us? Who is she?

Agatha gazed intently out to sea and up to the heavens. Her emotions floated up to the surface of her heart and sought for words to give them voice. She let out a long, slow sigh as she released her frustration and bowed her head to pray.

"There is not much I can say, just a plea for help. You are the God who turns bad around for good. I know that from my own life. Salamat. Thank you. Thank you. Help us to bring this girl back to life. Lord, please help her heal. Please help me understand *why* she came to us," she said aloud.

Agatha decided to take it a day at a time and trust that all these answers would somehow come to her in their own time. Agatha had faith for that. She could wait. Nothing in life is by accident. No. And life for this young girl is more than just survival.

There is a greater purpose in her being here. To discover that, we will all have to wait and see what comes. I only hope now that she lives through the night.

She turned back to prepare lunch. She shrugged her shoulders and wrinkled her brow. Agatha glanced up to the clouds as she left the beach. Under the filtered sunlight of the swaying palms, she paused and wiped the sweat from her face with the back of her hand, doing her best to straighten her wind-blown hair and put a smile back on her face.

CHAPTER FOURTEEN
THE HEALING

Around four pm, Agatha decided to try to wake and feed Antonia. She pulled up a rickety three-legged stool next to the bench in the living room and settled close to Antonia's head.

Peping and Solidad sat cross-legged on the floor nearby and watched as their mother dipped her fingers into a bowl of warm water in which she had cooked rice for lunch.

Beside her stool was a bucket filled with tepid water and a small white washcloth. Next to that was a half-coconut shell with freshly-squeezed coconut oil in it. All her supplies were ready.

Where shall I begin? Ayay!

She inhaled deeply.

Agatha gently lifted Antonia's head and held a small spoon to her parched lips. She slightly tilted the spoon so that several drops of rice water dribbled into Antonia's mouth. Most of the liquid escaped and slid down the side of her cheek and into her hair.

Agatha repeated this procedure many times without waking her patient. She then dipped two fingers into the bowl of coconut oil and swabbed Antonia's lips with the hope that the rich, oily liquid would begin to heal her wounds.

Then she pulled back the sheet from Antonia, and

brushed back her long tangled hair with her hand. Agatha wrung out the washcloth and gently dabbed away the dry salt residue from her forehead, neck, and arms.

Like a squadron of loving nursemaids, the children each took turns feeding her every hour until late into the evening. Antonia never even stirred in her sleep.

Pedro, the Saysons' oldest son, came home around midnight from a business trip to the big city of Cebu. He served as captain of the family's large, double-sailed boat that was chartered regularly to supply mangroves as firewood to Cebu bakeries.

Pedro removed his shoes, took off his heavy backpack, and quietly entered the house.

A muffled groan came from the corner of the room. As he searched for matches to light a candle so that he could see better, he stumbled over the three-legged stool that had been left in the middle of the room.

Pedro lit a candle on a small table and looked around. Someone was bundled up on the bamboo settee in the corner.

"Oy! Who's there?" What is going on here? Aaaah... I see. Mao na siya! *This is the girl they talked about at the harbor this afternoon.*

Pedro sat himself squarely on the stool and carefully studied the young woman curled up under a sheet on top of the stack of old woolen blankets. After a few minutes, he picked up the stool and set it down again closer to the makeshift bed to get a better look at this unexpected houseguest.

He pulled back the covers and laid his hand across Antonia's forehead. She burned with fever and tossed restlessly in her sleep. In horror, Pedro saw that the girl was close to death. He noticed the tangled shark's tooth necklace wrapped around her thin neck. Antonia groaned and whimpered often.

"Bevs... no! Where are you? Carlo! Carlo! Help!" she said in a barely audible voice.

She kicked and struggled against the sheet, which had become in her nightmare a crashing wave that pulled and pressed her down under the sea again and again.

"Ssshhhh," Pedro tenderly whispered. "It's okay, little sister... you are safe here."

He bent closely and continued to speak into her ear.

"You're on land, you are alive, and you are going to live"

He cautiously touched her frail shoulder. Antonia relaxed and was still again.

News of Antonia's arrival in Quezon had spread fast. Fishermen had been quick to tell Pedro as he docked his sailboat late that night that his mother, in the early morning hours of the day, had brought home a mostly-drowned young girl.

Bit by bit, the fishermen from the area had garnered every crumb of news to relate to Pedro. The men had made their own assumptions as to where she had come from and why she landed on a rock in Dinagat.

Although they had all experienced the huge typhoon that had hit their area two weeks ago, few would have ever guessed that Antonia's arrival was a result of that storm. It had been too long ago for survivors to wash up on shore now.

All the way home Pedro had contemplated the fate of this teen he had never met. Now that he sat at her bedside in the dark, he realized that she was much worse than he had dared to imagine.

Pity choked him, and he strained to see her features

through his tears. Shadows from the flickering candlelight danced over Antonia's body.

"Anod," he spoke quietly to Antonia in his dialect. "That's what I will call you. Anod -- *drifted*. For some reason you have drifted into our lives, and now it is up to us to find out why you are here. And to make sure you live again."

He clenched his fists and resolved to save this girl. He sat for a long time motionless in the dark room. Pedro had worked out at sea since he was a young boy, and he had seen his fair share of sun-damaged skin, but he had never seen such blistered skin or emaciated limbs.

He pulled the sheet tenderly under her chin, then blew out the candle and headed to his own room at the back of the house. He undressed in the dark.

In the morning I will find out the whole story.

As he lay upon his wooden bed, he pictured his fiancée, Bibay, in all her strength and self-assurance. She always held her head high, like a Spanish queen or one of the glamorous movie stars in the imported Hollywood films he had seen in a newly-built cinema in Cebu City. Bibay was everything to him, and he strove in his business to make her proud of him.

Pedro continually walked on eggshells to avoid her sharp temper and earn her praise. In his imagination, she loomed tall before him and looked down upon him as he lay in his bed. She was definitely a trophy, which he smugly paraded about the village. Bibay was perfect. Strong and perfect.

What will Bibay think of this...this... this problem we have now?

He wondered how he would manage their wedding plans now that this girl had come into their home. It was all so inconvenient.

Bibay's not going to be happy about this. I can just feel it. Maybe I don't have to tell her right away. Maybe the girl will die and...

His conscience shamed him for entertaining such dreadfully selfish thoughts.

What am I thinking?

Finally, sleep crept up on Pedro. Like Antonia, he dreamed of being lost in an angry, aggressive sea, alone on his big ship.

Outside, a gentle pitter-patter of many raindrops began to fall. The dry ground of Dinagat Island soaked up each fat drop of moisture like a thirsty child. The rain washed over the wide, dusty leaves of the banana trees around the Saysons' house.

A heavy rainfall arrived at daybreak. With it poured in a crew of curious neighbors and friends from all over Quezon who had received word about the girl who had drifted in from the great sea.

News had slithered out from the small barrio like a swarm of eels to every village round about. They wanted to see the abandoned girl Agatha had rescued on the shore. Or, according to the local gossip chain, the girl she had taken out of old Eduardo's fishing boat.

A plethora of people came from every surrounding town. Among those in the parade were overly-intrusive homemakers who would neglect their own children and chores for a few hours each morning over the next two weeks.

Farmers came on their way to their fields. Fishermen stopped by on their way to and from fishing. Elderly women huddled under their dripping umbrellas on their return from the open market. Curious groups of grade-school children skipped into the house on their way to class. A handful of meddling villagers with nothing better to do filled out the ranks of the watching throng.

Despite the downpour, people perched under the nearby trees and sheltered themselves from the rain with anything they could find to hold over their heads.

Antonia's arrival on their shores was the most exciting event to occur on the island in years. She came to town like a one-girl carnival. Her presence gave everyone something new to gossip about.

And everyone had his or her own opinion about this strange girl -- and about the Sayson family. According to the critical estimation of the busybodies in town, the Saysons were overly-protective of their new charge.

The crowds came early. They strained to peek through the cream curtains and squatted here and there where they found space, settling into the rain-soaked front yard as if they were waiting to get the best seat on the next jeepney that rolled into town.

When Narciso came out to feed his chickens, he was shocked as the mob barraged him with a host of personal questions. He could not tell who was more demanding: the cackling chickens that ran in circles underfoot in the pelting rain, or the visitors who clamored for Narciso's undivided attention.

This early-morning-visitor-scene would repeat itself daily for the next two weeks, when the novelty of Antonia's arrival began to wear off. The Saysons did not entertain the questions thrown at them from the yard; they mostly just smiled in a friendly way and returned inside their home.

Some neighbors, desperate for a peek at Antonia and determined to offer their unsolicited advice, became pushy and assertive, much to the dislike of Agatha and Pilar. The two sisters felt it was their responsibility to shelter the poor girl, and this daily scene had turned into a rather noisy, uncomfortable spectacle.

Antonia's strict feeding schedule brought a new sense of purpose to the family. Antonia slowly gained strength. Agatha hid the rice water for fear that Antonia would gorge herself and harm her shrunken stomach.

After a week, when she was able to sit upright, they began to give her bland, watery porridge, also on a controlled timetable so as not to over-feed her and cause stomach cramps.

Agatha was extremely cautious; she instinctively knew Antonia's needs. However, she welcomed the sound medical advice of a visiting nurse in Quezon whom Narciso had brought to their home one day. This lady had already heard about Antonia.

The nurse explained that Antonia showed many symptoms of heat stroke: a rapid pulse rate, disorientation, reoccurring high fevers, and difficulty breathing. Because of her extreme dehydration, Antonia would often vomit and had continual chest and abdominal pain, not to mention her shriveled skin.

For days on end, she would lay motionless and slip in and out of consciousness, leaving the family to fear that they had lost her. Then she would awake, drenched with sweat, only to find tear-stained faces huddled close to her own.

All four Sayson children hovered over Antonia and treated her as if she were a newborn in the family. They took turns feeding her, just as Agatha had taught them, caring for her open wounds and sun-scorched skin, which had begun to peel away.

They had never witnessed anything quite like the shedding of her skin. The old skin fell off in long strips and large dry patches. Like a molting snakeskin. Like newspaper burnt in fire until it was scorched, charred and black -- fragile and fine.

Every inch of her waif-like frame, including her scalp and the soles of her feet, shed its skin as the days passed. Underneath, the new skin was tender and pale.

Solidad especially found great joy keeping the night watch at Antonia's bedside; she felt like she had found a sister. The company of a teenage girl about her same age was the highlight of her day. She rushed home every day from high school, running the whole way, and plopped down to do her homework on the floor in front of Antonia.

She talked to Antonia as if she had known her all her life. Never mind that Antonia had no comment; Solidad rambled on and on about anything and everything. She simply assumed that Antonia was listening and understanding in her own way.

She poured out her secrets and the musings of her heart before her mute guest and found comfort in her calm presence and kind expressions.

Solidad shocked her family one day when she secretly took a pair of her mother's sewing scissors and, with great determination and a pounding heart, bluntly cut off all of Antonia's scraggly, bleached-out hair. Antonia's once waist-length locks lay in heaps on the floor like piles of dried, tangled seaweed.

Her new bob suited her delicate features and framed her petite face. Solidad tried to console her shocked mother and auntie that afternoon when they found her sweeping up all the hair.

"But *Ma*... this new cut is a cross between a flapper hairdo and Greta Garbo's style. We just have to finger-wave it into place!" she said.

Pedro had recently brought back American fashion

magazines from the big city of Cebu and, of course, they had landed in Solidad's eager hands. In those pages, she found hairstyles utterly different from the long, straight hair that Filipinas wore.

Solidad longed to go to the big cities, cities far bigger than Cebu or even Manila -- like New York, or Hollywood.

"But I know that having a haircut like a city girl is not the same as being one," Solidad said to Antonia as she admired her work. "Yeah, we're still island girls and will never be Western women with their long noses and pale skin."

She pulled at Antonia's short nose and snickered.

"Gwapa kaayo. Very beautiful."

Agatha and Pilar stood together in the doorway, hands resting on their hips, not knowing whether to scold Solidad for her brash act or praise her for her gutsiness. Antonia looked up meekly from under her newly-shorn coif and stifled a slight smile.

Upon seeing this grin, the two older women broke the awkward silence and laughed so hard they cried. Solidad had been holding her breath until she heard the laughter.

Losing all her hair -- her damaged hair -- was a small step for Antonia towards releasing her pain. She knew it was good to let go, and anyway, it would grow back healthy again.

Maybe my memories will heal in the same way.

Antonia realized the anguish in her heart as she sat propped up on the bed. She was only beginning to work through her heartache and the grief was often overwhelming. Seeing the pile of hair Solidad had swept up and taken away was good for her heart.

These were just some of the things that worried Agatha when she went to walk in the evenings out along the seashore or spoke in whispers with her husband behind closed doors. Her devoted caretaking for this new addition to their family certainly flowed out of a heart of compassion, but it also came from a mounting awareness in her that Antonia's arrival in their home was no accident.

Antonia said very little, but her countenance spoke volumes. A look of fear and shame mixed with gratitude and humility shone through her tender, swollen eyes. A deep sadness hung over her, and everyone sensed it, but no one mentioned it.

When dusk fell, Antonia would fall into an exhausted slumber. Agatha held firm to the hope that the girl was healing somewhere deep underneath her pain.

Antonia often woke at odd hours of the night with a muffled shriek of terror. Her rigid body would jerk up in her bed, and she would sit, staring wild-eyed into the darkness. The horror of her constant nightmares brought back the memories of her days alone in the ocean, struggling to survive. In the darkness the same words echoed over and over.

God, give me hope. God, give me hope.

During the long hours, she woke to the slashing of rain, and then she could not ignore the pain. Antonia would force herself to return to sleep, trying to forget the torment of watching her girlfriends be sucked into the sea.

As Antonia studied the constant torrents of rain outside the windows, she imagined that it was her own flood of tears shed for her great loss. The wind was increasing, a rhythmic moaning that rose to a howling and then screeching intensity. The cracks of lightning and booms of thunder reminded her of the wicked storm she survived at sea.

Antonia shivered.

Sheets of rain fell like an endless flow of grief. As she looked down at her own puny arms and legs, she felt like a broken soul covered with broken skin.

She still had no clear voice, as if she had lost it in the wind. Her words had no form as if they, too, had been buried out at sea with all of her friends. Antonia's throat felt scratchy as though sand had permanently lined her windpipes. Her mouth seemed raw and still swollen from the salt she had continually swallowed.

She moved her stiff body slowly, she often cried in silent sobs, and she shook uncontrollably day and night. The humid climate, steamy and sweltering despite the rain, did nothing at all to warm Antonia.

She was cold on the inside.

Antonia went on whispering the word "loto" between meals. Agatha could only guess that it was a plea of sorts, perhaps expressing Antonia's physical needs -- like hunger, thirst, cold, or pain. Whatever it meant, everyone in the village had learned Antonia's word, and the children chanted it in their games.

One day an old rice farmer, with his permanent toothless smile, showed up unexpectedly at their home and proudly explained that Antonia was saying "food" in Waray-Waray, a dialect from eastern Samar.

He stayed with the family all that day and shared his knowledge of words and expressions the family was longing to learn. Antonia perked up and smiled wearily back at the old man as he rattled away, clumsily using bits and pieces of her Waray-Waray dialect.

She could fully understand him. She lifted her eyebrows at times to respond to him when he asked her questions, but still no word came from her swollen lips.

Not until the old farmer left that evening at dusk, and she was alone with Pedro, did she break out of her silence. Pedro pulled out a chair from under the table and dragged it close to her bedside. It rasped along the wooden floor.

He picked up the small bowl of rice porridge on the round table next to Antonia and sat down. It was his turn to spoon-feed Antonia, and he was quiet and pensive, not his normal jolly self.

"Oops! Sorry, Anod... I am so clumsy tonight."

He had spilled half the porridge on his lap and was attempting to clean up his mess.

"I don't know what's wrong with me. I guess I have a lot of troubles on my mind."

"You know, Pedro, my name is Antonia," she said softly to him as he leaned over to wipe up another spoonful of porridge, which he had just spilled near his foot.

He bolted straight up and smiled brightly at her, speechless in surprise.

"Marasa an iyo luto. Salamat. Your food is delicious; thank you," she said, using some of the Wary-Wary phrases that the old man had taught the family that day.

Wide-eyed, Pedro smiled even more.

"I think I am finding my voice again," she spoke softly with her head bowed.

"Well, Anod... it's about time! We have all been worried that you might never talk to us. Antonia, eh? Such a pretty name."

"Yes. Thank you. My friends call me Tonya. My parents named me after my grandmother on Suluan where I was born."

"*Suluan? Really?* You come from Suluan? Oh my goodness! The small island east of Samar, the one with the lighthouse? I have heard of it from my fishermen friends who sail north of here. So that's where you come from, Tonya!"

Antonia sat still as tears slowly rolled down her cheeks. "Oo. Yes. That is my home." the words out loud -- Antonia, Suluan, home -- brought Antonia's pain to the surface with a stinging freshness.

"Anod, you're crying again." Pedro was suddenly nervous. "Here, eat a bit more and get some strength."

He reached again for the spoon and dipped it in the warm porridge.

He slowly lifted it to her lips and said, "Do you know what I think? I think...uh... I think your healing has begun tonight."

She stared blankly at the wrinkled skin on her hands, her fingers entwined together on her lap. She swallowed hard and nodded her head up and down. More tears began to fall.

Carefully, he reached out and touched her shoulder. At his touch, Antonia began to weep wildly, her hands covering her face.

She has borne this for weeks, he thought, *ever since she arrived.*

Pity rose and choked him.

"Maayo. Very good. It's good to let go of your pain. Tears are good. Now we will talk again tomorrow," he said softly.

Pedro realized Antonia was overwhelmed. He finished feeding her in polite silence, placed the spoon back in the bowl, and set it on the small table near her bed. He looked at the tear-stained face and cropped hair of the helpless girl before him.

"Maayong gabii. Good-night," he said. "Your sleep will be good tonight."

He looked steadily into her swollen black eyes. Then he excused himself and disappeared into the semi-darkness without lighting a candle in the room, and Antonia could hear the hushed whispers of the Sayson family in the back of the house. She imagined that Pedro shared the news of her newly-disclosed name, of Suluan, and of her first few words.

Perhaps Pedro is right. My healing has begun.

How pleasant it was to finally have someone to talk to instead of only speaking to herself and to the waves of the sea in her dreams.

CHAPTER FIFTEEN
THE HEROES

In the last month since the storm, Suluan had become a place of utter confusion. Gone was the customary tranquility of simple native life under the shelter of lanky palms. The trees still stood erect like protective sentinels around the center of town and grew thick, side-by-side, covering the rest of the island with their lush green foliage.

They looked like majestic armor bearers, but they could not defend the town from its grief. Even gentle breezes, which normally blew happily through the trees and hanging laundry, were unable to blow away the disturbance that infiltrated the air.

The rainy season arrived prematurely on Suluan, just as it had on Dinagat Island, where Antonia now resided. The jungle floor drank in the moisture. The ground was sodden and brown due to the drenching rain. After a sudden shower, large puddles in the roads shone like pools of melted chocolate.

Shrill gusts of wind blasted through the village. The stormy weather left nothing secure, often making it difficult to walk from one place to another. The turbulent waves at sea forced the fishermen of Suluan to stay home more often than they wanted.

Storms shrieked outside as well as resident within the homes of the six young men who had crawled upon the shore, barely alive. The fight to save their lives still raged full force, spilling into the very family fiber of Suluan. Not one family on the two mile-long island was unaffected by the tragedy of the capsized boat. Some, however, were suffering more than others.

Outside, the tall coconut trees swayed violently. The whoosh of long leaves and the banging of loosened metal roofs filled the chilly air, a pulsating accompaniment to the tumult of the wind. Mam Salud and Papa Beni were still panting as they arrived at the home of Peter's father, drenched from the rain despite the wide umbrella-like banana leaf they each carried over their heads.

They could all hear the pounding of the sea. It seemed impossible that anything living could stand up to this assault of wind and water. The two ran barefoot and splashed through puddles the size of small ponds; their clothes were wet and stuck to their skin.

Never mind. There were more important things to talk about with the parents of the five surviving and the three dead boys than the current precipitation.

"I'm at a total loss of what to do," said the mother of Jhun and Ofelia, and then she began to weep.

Mam Salud nodded as if she understood, but secretly she was dreadfully confused as well and afraid for her own grandson, Carlo. He had suffered constant seizures every day for the past several weeks. When he was not rolling on the floor in convulsions, unbearable headaches rendered him helpless.

As Suluan's wise and knowing barangay captain who had solved most of the island's minor problems up until now, Mam Salud had no advice to offer any parent in the room; there was no eagerness in the whispers around her today. They had all lost faith in recovering their sons and daughters.

She meekly looked to Papa Beni for advice and

searched his haggard face for any glimmer of hope. He gave her a slight reassuring nod and his familiar awkward smile. His crooked teeth protruded beyond his lips a bit. He slowly began to speak.

"Everyone, please listen. We have to realize that these boys suffered extreme exhaustion and mental torment during the typhoon in their brave attempt to find help for the girls. The news that we were unable to find any wreckage from the boat and no sign of our precious girls has hit them hard. It is much worse than I had expected...than we all expected. I am so sorry. I fear that we are going to lose them all. These are our boys — they are all of our sons. Our children mean everything to us."

He bowed his head.

Sobs came from every corner of the room.

The father of Amado walked over to Papa Beni, put his arm around his shoulders, and stared at their bare feet on the wooden floor. Their boys had grown up together, had been best of friends, and had swum together for hours in a typhoon, then risked their lives to save others. No words of comfort, no speeches -- nothing seemed appropriate as the parents grieved in silence.

Mam Salud was as kind under pressure as she was smart. She spoke haltingly, but clearly and without tears.

"I believe that in our sadness we all understand that we are parents of very brave heroes. I cannot speak for all of you here today, but for myself, I could not be more proud of these boys, all nine of them, who demonstrated courage and strength beyond their young years."

The sobs quieted as Mam Salud continued.

"Our grandchildren and their children, and their children to come -- all who ever hear of this island -- will know of the testimony of these young men. Their loyalty and sacrifice bring honor to all of your family names. They are no longer children; they are true men, extraordinary individuals who loved their friends and their home more than they loved and valued their own lives. They have left us a legacy of kindness."

Salud paused and gathered herself.

"We can all rest assured that the six girls died with the assurance that these boys of ours gave their best for them. The three young men who suffered and died on their way home to Suluan have been spared the torment we now witness among those who survived. I can only hope and pray, for the sake of the boys and for all of you that they do not suffer much longer."

"It's unbearable," the mother of Alfredo spoke out.

Her face clouded over like a sudden thunderstorm.

"Alfredo blames himself for the death of his brother. Nothing we say can stop his crying or pacify his guilt. It keeps him up all night. He gets so agitated and then leaves the house at all hours; he roams the island and weeps uncontrollably. We just don't know what to do for him to ease his pain."

"Rey, who has always been so positive and full of life," said his father in a soft voice, "has not spoken a word since he arrived. He doesn't react to our questions and barely eats or sleeps. What are we to do to help him? We can't lose him! Yeah, we have all our girls with us, but he's our only son."

Then Peter's father came to stand at Papa Beni's side. He stood very straight, lifted his head, and looked slowly at each couple. His heart thumped loudly in his chest. He took in a long breath. Then he exhaled slowly and began.

"You all know that my wife passed away years ago, and I've raised my Pete alone. I thought the other day, when he was lying on his bed with a high fever and could barely breathe, that I'm thankful to have had his company all these years. He's been the best son a father could ask for… " Osting's voice broke and trailed off into silence.

"I wonder about Daisy's parents in Guiuan," Papa Beni said. "They expected her to come home. The wedding was scheduled weeks ago, and since then no boats have sailed between our islands. They must be terribly concerned about their beautiful girl." He stopped short. "The weather has finally cleared, and I plan to go in the next day and meet with her family. I'm sure they know that something terrible has happened."

At that, both Beni and Salud broke down and wept. They had loved their charming future daughter-in-law ever since Carlo had first brought her home to Suluan to meet them last year. Carlo was intensely grieving her loss. He, too, suffered through long, sleepless nights and refused to eat.

With bowed heads, the parents took leave from one another. They ran through the rain against a sudden gusting wind to the safety of their own homes.

As the months passed, each boy succumbed to his inevitable death. Old and young mourned their loss -- grieving alone in silence, and together as a village. Simple caskets of wood carried the boys' bodies beneath the soft Suluan earth. Some of the caskets landed empty in their holes in honor of those children who had never returned home.

These heroes of the sea were laid to rest beneath the island soil just behind the village center in a small cemetery. The residents of Suluan did not know then that the strange symptoms exhibited by these young men were textbook reactions caused by extreme conditions and exposure to the elements.

Ignorance spread the rumors that the boys were insane. They ran wild around the island of Suluan until their death. They had suffered dehydration, shock, cold, exhaustion, and grief -- physical conditions and emotions simply more than they could bear.

The parents of the young men as well as the six young women, who were believed to have perished at sea, sought solace in one another's presence. Antonia's two-story home close to the seaside was a regular gathering place for the families of Bevs, Ofelia, Perla, and her cousin Lita.

Hope that the families struggled to maintain for weeks seeped from their hearts. Finally, overwhelmed with sadness, they grudgingly accepted the cruel fact that they would never see their teenage girls again.

They were all tired. So tired.

Agony over the loss of their girls had worn them out, aged them. But a question gnawed at them and hung heavy in the air. Why had no one noticed the inclement weather on the morning the teens set sail for Guiuan?

Everyone was too polite to broach the subject publicly. They had already lost so much; adding shame to their grief would have capsized their hearts altogether.

CHAPTER SIXTEEN
THE RECOVERY

Bibay, the fiancée of Pedro, tapped softly on the front door. Behind her stood her companion, her neighbor and best friend, Luz Rodrigo.

"Maayo... Hello. Pssst. Maayo. Is anyone home?"

The girls knocked again and again with no response. They kicked off their shoes on the top step and proceeded bare-footed into the house.

This was the first time Bibay had come to visit Pedro since Antonia had arrived. She knew about the rescue of this Suluan girl, but her work at home on the other side of town kept her too busy to come to the Saysons. Pedro had not been to see her since Antonia had arrived, either, and that had left Bibay feeling more than neglected.

No one was in the room as the two young women tiptoed in and looked around. For a few seconds, Bibay stood transfixed by the scene before her. Next to Antonia's empty bed sat piles of neatly-folded woolen blankets stacked in the corner of the room.

On a small table was a bouquet of miniature wild roses. A hair comb, a native woven pi-pi fan, and an empty coconut bowl lay on the floor under the slatted sofa bed. The cream curtains flapped in the breeze.

Luz and Bibay followed the sound of laughter coming from the back of the house. They smelled moist earth and sweet fruit, with a trace of smoke. Out the door they went, past the dirty kitchen outside, and into the small fenced-in backyard.

Luz remained near the dirty kitchen and peered into the yard as Bibay ventured out farther to greet the Saysons. She stood tall, with her hands firmly set on her hips. Her narrow eyes were set under thin arched brows. She watched with hostility as the entire Sayson family assisted a girl, who she assumed to be Antonia, to stand and walk.

No one noticed Bibay's arrival.

Peping held Antonia up by her left elbow, and Pedro guided her by her right hand. Quirino slowly followed behind them with his arms protectively outstretched, just in case she fell backwards. Narciso, Agatha, Solidad, and Pilar led the way. They cheered and clapped. Bibay stiffened at the sight of Pedro holding the skinny girl's hand.

Pedro had bound thick pads of fresh, soft banana leaves around Antonia's feet to protect the new skin on her soles, since it was not yet tough enough to walk on. In spite of her tender feet, the entire family had concluded it was time for her to get out of her bed and start to move again. They had begged her to try.

Antonia bent over slightly as she walked, and had a difficult time balancing and moving forward. Every move seemed painful. Her mincing steps were met with more cheers and applause.

"You are walking!" said Narciso.

"See, I told you she was ready," said Pilar.

"Yeah, Tonya! Keep going! Come on, you can do it!" said Solidad.

Bibay cleared her throat, and everyone looked up to see her standing a few feet away. Her face was both hard and lovely at the same time. She wore a clean cotton dress of pale icy blue, which fell right below her knees. A crisp blue bow, neatly tied at the nape of her neck, held together a long, thick ponytail of shiny black hair that hung halfway down her back. Her hair was pulled back taut away from her face, emphasizing her high forehead and delicate bone structure.

What no one could see was something inside of her turning a deep shade of bitter. She stood stiffly straight and looked at them all somewhat uncomfortably. Bibay wished that all the family attention was focused on her. Normally she was the one everyone fussed over.

"Maayong buntag tanan. Good morning, everybody," she said brusquely.

Her eyes met Antonia's gaze, but Bibay's sour expression didn't change. She had no compassion for the young girl who must learn to walk again. It was Pedro, and Pedro alone, whom she wished to see. But his focus was completely on Antonia even then, and not at all on Bibay.

He didn't even look up to greet her. Quirino left his post as rear-guard and came over to greet both of the guests properly. He disappeared inside the house and came back with some freshly-squeezed lemony calamansi juice, sweetened with much sugar, and several squares of buko cake that his Auntie Pilar had brought over that morning for breakfast. He led them to a small wooden table and chairs close to the door and helped them take their seats.

"You finally get to meet our new little sister. This is Antonia!" He pointed out to the garden and took a seat.

Bibay raised her thinly-plucked eyebrows, smiled weakly up at him, leaned back in her chair, and folded her arms tightly across her chest. She felt her face starting to heat up. Her thoughts raced from the scene in the yard to her last argument with Pedro.

She clenched her teeth and flashed a fake smile in the

direction of Antonia. Her cold hard stare bore down on Antonia from across the yard. If her eyes could speak they would say that they didn't care at all.

"She's... um... walking for the first time today?" asked Bibay with sarcasm in her voice.

"Oo. Yes. We've wanted to get her out of bed for so long, and I think today we've all had a breakthrough," said Quirino.

"She's certainly been here *a long time*, hasn't she?" Bibay mocked.

Quirino stood abruptly and looked down at her. Her head was tilted back, her lips parted, and her dark eyes flashed with anger. He could see the pulse beating beneath her smooth chocolate skin. Bibay was upset; that was obvious.

Not wanting to be impolite, he controlled his disgust and didn't answer Bibay. Instead, he excused himself and hastened back to join his brothers in the yard, leaving the girls to themselves.

Agatha and her sister both noticed that Pedro was not about to drop his job with Antonia, so they dutifully came to the table to keep the girls company. Bibay sat rigidly in her chair and didn't say much. She glanced around the yard and looked at everything except over at Pedro, not wanting him to think she cared.

She sighed loudly and murmured to Luz, "I just don't see what all the fuss is about. I mean, she's *just* a sickly girl they found on the shore. I'm sure she'll be just fine and then they can send her back to her home... *wherever that is.*"

Agatha opened her mouth to breathe. It was only then she realized that she'd held her breath, afraid to make a sound. Sitting there at the table with Bibay was uncomfortable for her. She observed her future daughter-in-law out of the corner of her eye and did not like what she saw or heard.

The atmosphere at the table grew tense. Agatha sat motionless. Her faced flushed as anger rose and strangled her words. Pilar was restless and quiet. Agatha cleared her throat and stood up.

"Excuse me, please. I need to go check on something in the house."

With her head lowered, she disappeared from the backyard.

That morning the Sayson family, including Pilar, had eaten breakfast earlier than usual. Pilar had come knocking an hour before the sun rose. Her loosely-braided hair, pulled back and away from her face, hung below her shoulders. She had quickly thrown on a green button-downed dress. Of the three simple dresses she owned, it fit her slim frame the best.

She came with warm buko cake, rolls of sweetened sticky rice, flavored with anise seed and wrapped in banana leaves, and a plate of still-hot fried banana fritters.

The large bamboo-slatted table already had a big wooden bowl of steaming rice sitting in the middle of it. Next to it was a long dish of salted fish, a platter of fried eggs, plump mangoes split open around their long pit and arranged on a white plate, a large wedge of fragrant jackfruit in a bowl, and a pot of native hot cocoa. The table was set with the hope that Antonia would be joining them today.

They were all eager for Antonia to wake up so they could hear her speak. It felt like Christmas morning! Pedro repeated everything Antonia had told him the night before, and as he was explaining, he retrieved a small map of the Philippines from his backpack.

He pointed to Suluan far east of the big island of

Samar. They stared in amazement as he traced a path through the ocean from Dinagat Island up to Suluan.

"I estimate that her home is at least 45 miles north of us, maybe about ten hours by boat. I am very eager to find out how in heaven's name she arrived on our shore. It's crazy that she landed here without a ship, without anyone else with her. She was out in water with incredibly strong currents -- and sharks."

When Antonia stirred in the living room, the family bolted to her bedside, but no one dared say a word. Wide eyed, they watched her every move. She slowly sat up, smoothed her tousled mop of hair, and untangled the shark tooth necklace twisted around her neck. Surprised, she looked up at each face, smiled shyly, and said a soft hello.

The room filled with wild applause, and she felt her face flush warm from embarrassment. Solidad could not contain her joy. She jumped on top of her friend and embraced her.

"May I have the honor of escorting you to the table this morning?" Narciso asked politely. "We have prepared a breakfast in your honor."

She nodded, and he scooped down, picked her up, and carried her out to the kitchen in the back. The rest of Antonia's entourage followed along behind them. They took their places at the table and bowed their heads to give thanks.

Agatha had made Antonia a small bowl of rice porridge, as she did every day.

"Today, my dear, you may eat a bit of mango and jackfruit. I think the fruit is easy enough to digest. It will give you more strength."

Antonia smiled. The aroma of the food encircled her, as did the holy laughter of family. She took it all in with a reassuring and nostalgic sense of being home. She couldn't help but think of her own older brothers, her mother and father, her grand-parents, all her aunties and uncles and the cousins who had regularly filled their table back on Suluan. Being a part of the Sayson family felt like home. Her porridge had never tasted as delicious as it had today.

Breakfast went long, dragged out by the interrogation that took place around the table. Each one took a turn asking a question that he or she had ached to know since Antonia had washed up on their shores weeks ago. They spoke slowly and waited patiently for her to answer.

Together, the family helped Antonia unravel the confusing near-death journey to their home, unwrapping her past gently, like a delicate package. They had all decided the night before not to overwhelm her with too much at once. However, one answer led to another question and to another.

This was a morning of a dozen breakthroughs! Until now, Antonia had been a mystery to the Sayson family. Her arrival had raised so many questions, not only in their home, but also throughout all Quezon. Spending time with her this morning, hearing her small voice and incredible story of survival, made today a special, holy day.

Stories of Antonia's life on Suluan: her family, schooling, and friendships, as well as the tragic sailboat ride into the unexpected typhoon, tumbled out of her heart – with tears and trembling. Her silence had been broken, and now her heart unlocked. The family hung on her every word.

Agatha shook her head and marveled. This young girl had lost so much and had been so brave. This traumatic drama gave the small loss in Agatha's own life a whole new perspective as she recalled her separation from her own family back on Leyte.

When Antonia explained about the huge shark that had not only warded off the school of hungry sharks, but also rescued her and brought her to the shore on Dinagat, awe filled the room. The boys had heard stories of these huge whale sharks, as they called them, and Narciso had seen one from a distance while swimming as a young boy, but they had never heard of a shark that rescued anyone.

"Actually, dear Antonia, these whale sharks with the enormous mouths only eat plankton, so you were safe, my dear," said Narciso.

Pedro, Peping and Quirino all nodded in agreement.

Peping added, "But still, I'd never want to meet one alone in the ocean! What if he *was* hungry and thought I was a piece of big plankton!"

Everyone laughed. Antonia gave a sigh of relief and hung her head.

Agatha slowly took a sip of her hot cocoa, set down her cup, and looked directly at Antonia.

"I believe that you experienced a true miracle out at sea. Your life was spared and it was spared for a very good reason."

"God sent that fish to you ... like He sent the whale to Jonah!" said Solidad.

She was enthralled with the details and asked to hear the whole shark rescue account again, starting with the storm.

"He brought you to us, didn't He?" she exclaimed.

Agatha continued, "Dear Tonya, you realize, don't you, that you were not alone out in that big ocean? You had faith; you didn't give up hope, even when all hope was gone. I think I can speak for all of us here -- the good Lord saw fit to save your precious life and to bring you to our shores. We are very thankful to know you. I am *especially* blessed to have been the one to find you. You've made such wonderful progress, and in no time you'll be running around and we'll be able to bring you home to your dear island of Suluan."

Antonia's eyes glistened with fresh tears of joy. "I miss my family dearly," she whispered.

"I think our beautiful young mermaid from Suluan needs to get ready for the day. Why don't we women clear all this food and you men escort her back to get her things? Solidad, you can help her wash up after you help me with the table. Peping, please go fetch water so that Tonya can wash. Quirino, please bring your mother some more fire-wood for the kitchen. Pedro, don't you need to pack your things for your trip to Cebu this evening?" Pilar spoke quickly as she organized the Sayson household.

Agatha sat contently and smiled as she watched Peping pick up Antonia and bring her back to the living area.

So that is how she landed on our beach. First on the rock and then brought to our shore by the fishermen. That is why I found her alone in the boat. Now it all makes sense.

A few hours later, she had the idea to bring Antonia out into the back garden to get her up on her feet and try walking for the first time. This was a holiday in the Sayson home -- until Bibay and Luz appeared.

Their arrival had put a damper on all the fun in the yard. Agatha and Pilar both sensed the anxiety that Bibay brought with her. Bibay's jealous eyes saw Pedro's attention to help Antonia as a personal threat. As a result, Bibay did not stay long.

She politely thanked them all for the delicious cake and drink but excused herself soon after she arrived, explaining that she had work to do in her mother's sari-sari store at home.

The young women stood, waved their good-byes to

the group that surrounded Antonia, and quietly left. She and Luz disappeared around the side of the house, tramped through the garden full of noisy chickens and ducks, and headed back home in a huff.

It was only in the late afternoon as Pedro packed up his supplies and backpack to leave for his ship that his thoughts turned to Bibay.

If she's mad... well, I will just have to live with that. I had other, more important things to do, than to just sit and listen to her and Luz chatter about themselves all morning.

Numbly, he folded another shirt and stuffed it into his bag.

He couldn't figure out his own feelings, but something just didn't sit right. He felt frustrated and at the same time angry. He didn't like being controlled by Bibay's temper, sharp tongue, and her subtle way of expressing her dislikes.

But Pedro had never openly objected to her mannerisms, for he wanted to avoid conflict at all cost. He had definite ideas of what for him constituted a suitable wife. She was beautiful. She did love him. Everyone in town said they were meant for each other.

Somehow, however, he felt very happy to pack up his bags and have some time away at sea for the next few days. Life with Bibay was overly complicated, and he needed to escape. He had to distribute a lot of mangrove wood to the bakeries in Cebu City, and he wanted to take off before any more rain fell.

In the days that followed, the women of the house (including Pilar, of course) spent long hours on the floor at the bedside of Antonia. They listened intently to her stories of her home and of each friend she'd lost at sea. They heard of her best friend, Bevs, of the shy and beautiful Perla, of her strict cousin Lita, and of the kindness of her friend Ofelia.

Antonia told of the love story between her dearest childhood playmate, Carlo, and the strong, winsome girl from Guiuan, Daisy. When she was not talking with the women, she entertained the people from town who dropped by to hear her story of the whale shark rescue. It was such an amazing tale that both young and old sat mesmerized and listened with rapt attention.

Especially the little girls. They crawled all over Antonia; they played with her hair and massaged her feet while she spoke. They brought her juice and little sacks of warm pandesal rolls from their mothers. They bombarded her with millions of questions.

When she opened her eyes in the morning, she would hear them giggle and catch them peeking in at her from outside the windows, waiting for her to awaken. They would have worn her out had they not been so charming in their innocence.

To these little girls, Antonia from Suluan was a heroine. For she was young, had endured a typhoon out at sea, had floated without food for over two weeks, had ridden a whale shark like a storybook princess, and she had survived it all!

They loved her cheery teenage smile as much as they loved to listen to her story of adventure being lost out at sea. Antonia began to see that these little Filipinas looked to her for inspiration, and she did not take that lightly. She often found herself telling the children *never* to get scared of anything -- *never* to give up -- *never* to stop trying -- and *always* to love their moms and dads.

Agatha often told her that through these girls she would find something to live for again. Agatha was right.

"What's that sharks tooth around your neck?" one of the smallest girls asked Antonia one afternoon. "Who gave it to you? Did Ate Agatha?"

"Wala. No," Antonia said with a laugh.

She tugged at the worn leather strap that held the shiny tooth.

"A little girl from Suluan, the island where I came from, gave this to me. She's about as big as you are, Inday, and just as sweet, and she is my little cousin, Rosalyn. This necklace was my good luck present from her before we left the island."

The girls around Antonia clapped and all wanted to touch the real shark's tooth. They screamed and squealed as they did.

"Oy, Ate, good thing the sharks didn't eat you on your trip to our island. You must have been so special that they all decided not to bite. And then that big, big fat fish with spots came and rescued you and brought you to our place, di ba? Isn't that right, Ate Tonya? You are a present to us here on Dinagat," the little girl said.

All the children around her nodded.

Antonia blushed and hugged the girl and whispered into her ear, "You are my present, too, Inday!" Then she turned to all the girls and said, "Children, you need to always remember that God sees you, no matter where you are, or how far away from home you travel -- He is with you. Keep trusting Him; let Him be your hope and your song, even in the darkest night."

Antonia tugged again on the shark tooth and felt its sharp point; inside she cringed and pushed the pain of her loneliness deeper. Then she continued.

"Even if you are lost, even if you can't find your way home, or if you are in danger, just cry out to the Lord, and He will bring you to safety. He knows every fish in the sea and every bird in the sky. And of course He loves you more than all these, doesn't He?"

The girls' eyes were wide with wonder, and they hung

on Antonia's every word. If only Antonia could embrace these truths as easily as the children did. Of course God had heard her cry and had rescued her, but why was she still struggling with such grief?

Pedro decided one day that it would be good for Antonia to get out of the house and to get some fresh air and sunshine. He had noticed that in the last few days she had been more quiet than usual and had a difficult time looking him in the eye when he spoke to her. That concerned him.

There was no rain in the sky that day, so he suggested that they go out to the shoreline behind the house. He knew she had not been near the sea since she arrived and felt like it was time to help her return and face her fears. At least that is what his Auntie Pilar had suggested to him late yesterday evening.

He lifted Antonia out of her bed, scooped up one of the blankets so she would have something to sit on, plopped his old straw hat on her head, and headed out the door. He found a quiet spot along the shore under a big shady palm tree away from the possibility of direct sun. Before setting her down, he spun her around until they were both dizzy.

He whispered in her ear, "Day, I am so happy for you! You're healing."

Then he settled her on the blanket and turned to leave. He had repair work to do on his ship and needed to finish the loading before departing.

"Peping will be here in an hour to bring you home. Now don't go running off anywhere, okay, Anod?"

She smiled. "Salamat, manong Pedro."

But her memories cut in, ruining the moment.

Carlo used to twirl me around just like that.

She immediately lost her smile.

Pedro had walked about one hundred yards when he stopped and turned back to the shore. He stood silently behind her, hands stuffed deep in his pockets, and struggled with his words. He saw her smile lose its sparkle.

"You know, Anod, you don't have to suffer in silence. Don't you know that your heart can feel like an anchor when you keep everything inside? You're like an island, a bit like Suluan... but you don't have to be. I'm just a word away, if ever you feel like talking. Okay, little sister?"

She did not respond, and he turned and walked away slowly.

Diffused light flickered upon her lap as the palm leaves far above her head swayed back and forth like a hula dancer. Content to be alone but fearful to be so close to the sea again, Antonia fidgeted with her blanket and her skirt, trying to distract herself.

The endless blue ocean was daunting, no longer her friend as it had once been. As she looked out from under the brim of Pedro's hat at the hazy sun, her partial smile turned to scorn. Even its weak glare still made her eyes burn, so she looked away. Fractions of light danced on ripples of water -- sparkling, reflecting. She saw only her endless days at sea.

A tug-of-war ripped her heart in two. Her calloused heart wanted to open up, but painful memories of the storm that had brought her to this place held her captive. Recollections of treasured friendships, now buried in the deep sea of her grief, remained distant.

The days of wishing and wondering were far away, back on Suluan. Antonia sighed aloud. Her secret dreams were hidden away in the cave up on the cliffs of Suluan, loves in her life now dead in the ocean.

Oh Bevs, I still think of you each time I see the sun and the sea. I didn't want a day without you -- but somehow I'm living through yet another one.

Evil waters had ripped her friends out into eternity. Forceful waves and currents had torn her away from her happy life on Suluan. Anger rose within her as she studied the tiny grains of sand sprinkled around her blanket's edge. Nothing made sense. She felt her jaws tighten and her teeth clench. She felt old, as if she had aged a decade in a matter of a few weeks.

Where is my home now? Where do I really belong? Has life continued without me on Suluan? What do I do when I return? Is this how life is supposed to change for me? Maybe it is how Mario told us... we choose. I certainly have my independence now. But letting go of all my friends... of Carlo, of Bevs... of Suluan. That was not my choice.

A noisy black bird chirped overhead and then took off suddenly. He flapped his wings hard as he left. Fishermen returned from their long night at sea. The familiar sounds of island life surrounded her -- so similar to the sounds of Suluan that they were somehow a comfort.

She took a deep breath and looked up to the water's edge, where the crabs scampered among the many shells and dodged the tide, as if they were playing tag with the water that washed ashore.

Why am I the only girl who survived? What if the boys never made it back to Suluan? Maybe they would have been here with me had they not tried to swim back home to get help. Maybe Carlo survived and he's worried sick about Daisy. But Daisy is gone.

Antonia still suffered from homesickness, though she was ashamed to admit it to her loving new family. She felt emotionally ill-equipped to confront this intimidating new life. Guilt-ridden thoughts obsessively plagued her waking hours.

More than regret, more than sadness, her heart ached

so intensely that she suspected it had drowned at sea --
but somehow it kept beating as life kept marching
forward. Like the crabs in front of her, she ran in and out
of her own holes of doubt and fear.

Peping came in an hour, just as Pedro had promised,
and brought her back to the house. She left her many
unanswered questions at the shore along with the sand
she had brushed off her feet.

I do have a choice about what I bring home with me, she
mused.

In the days that followed, Peping and Quirino took it
upon themselves to teach Antonia how to walk again.
Their patience and humor made the challenging task the
highlight of each day. By the time that Pedro had
returned from his business in Cebu, she was walking
alone.

Relearning to walk like a child humbled her. She had
to find her feet, depend on people she barely knew, and
trust herself. These were hard lessons to learn all over
again.

*There probably is a lot more I have to learn... and un-learn. I
have to give up what I am, and what I have had, to become the
person I must be. I cannot go through life just floating along.*

CHAPTER SEVENTEEN
THE LAUNDRY

Away from the shoreline of Dinagat, where the sky met the sea, dark clouds hovered on the eastern horizon. It looked like rain would reach the area in several hours, but there was no immediate threat of a storm, according to radio reports, as Pedro pushed off from the dock. He was captain of a large double-sailed boat that belonged to his father, Narciso Sayson.

With his crew of four men, he spent a good part of the afternoon loading the mangrove timber into the boat's wide hull. Tired and hot from the hours of backbreaking work, the five men welcomed the cool breezes from the Habagat winds and a chance to rest.

They skipped over the small whitecaps and headed southwest toward the setting sun. Soon they would maneuver through the Surigao Strait and then around the tip of Leyte, then north around the island of Bohol and then finally westward to Cebu.

The waters were still full of small bangkas that paddled peacefully back to shore. These low-lying, cheerfully-painted canoes with long extended outriggers on each side brightened the evening scene. Several people hunched in each boat, swathed in long sleeves and cloths tied around their heads that protected them from the sun and wind.

As the sky darkened, the crew had to keep a constant

lookout for small fishing boats that ran their unseen trawl lines and nets through the waters, because many of them carried no lights.

Trips like these kept Pedro away from home sometimes more than half a month. Once on the island of Cebu, he would travel to different roadside bakeries that had ordered the mangrove wood to use in their ovens. All this time away from home gave him plenty of opportunity to think.

No angry waves sputtered below him, but he could not quiet or escape the storm inside. He felt unsettled about his upcoming marriage to Bibay. Ever since his new little sister, "Anod," had arrived, his focus and his affections for Bibay had shifted.

Despite the problems Antonia had brought with her, she had given energy to their home as well as a sense, not of perfection, but of life. He was happy for the first time in years.

Now he did not know what to do, and it made him angry. He looked up at the great sky with the hope that it might bring him some kind of heavenly wisdom or revelation.

Perhaps getting out to sea will clear my mind. I need answers, he thought.

He scanned the horizon and banged his clenched fist repeatedly on the wooden rail of his sailboat.

Meanwhile, Pilar and Agatha fought their own battle at home. Agatha had decided that she did not want her son to marry Bibay. Since Pedro had begun courting her, Agatha and Pilar had had many distressful conversations about the pros and cons of her eldest son's serious relationship. But Agatha did not want to nag her son, nor did she want to steal the pride he seemed to have found in being with such a lovely young lady.

Admittedly, Bibay was a known beauty on their island, and many young men had tried to court her before Pedro asked her father for her hand. Since that time, however, Agatha had witnessed how Pedro's unhappiness had grown. He was often irritable and overly sensitive after spending time with Bibay. Agatha was also moody, and when Agatha was not happy, neither was Pilar.

The women began to scheme together. At first, their idea started out as a joke, but after they spent hours talking about everything, their fantasies blossomed into a master plan to stop the wedding.

The only problem was reconciling the love they shared for Pedro, whom they saw as grown up able to make his own decisions, with the need to step in and protect him.

Not only did Agatha dislike Bibay as a future daughter-in-law, but she had also become fixated on Antonia. The longer Antonia was under their roof and in her family's care, the more she grew to love her.

She saw herself reflected in this young girl in many ways. Agatha could understand the agony Antonia felt because she was far from her home and her loved ones on Suluan. She, too, had experienced extreme loneliness over the years.

The women appreciated Antonia's deep love for family and for home, her skill in the garden, and her neatness around the house. Most of all, the way she cared for the small children in the village greatly impressed not only Agatha, but Narciso, too. Agatha knew young Antonia would someday be a wonderful mother.

Unlike Bibay, who was brash and often temperamental, Antonia was soft spoken, sweet, and a natural peace-maker. Even among her own four children, Antonia had a calming effect. They loved to gather around her to talk and always left encouraged; she was already part of the family.

"Just you remember," Pilar reminded Agatha, although it was not necessary to do so, "that God brought Antonia into the Sayson family. He must have some plan in all of this!"

It made sense to the women, so they convinced themselves that what they were about to do was perfectly fine and in order. No one ever mentioned the word "match-making," but that was exactly what they planned to do.

Agatha was content to leave the details to Pilar, who had a clever idea. She took out a small piece of paper and, in her best handwriting, wrote a lengthy love letter to Antonia and signed it with Pedro's name. She tiptoed out of the house, folded the paper, and stuck it in the side pocket of Antonia's skirt as it hung on the clothesline at the side of the house.

Pilar continued on to her home next door, guilt-free about what she had just done. She never said a word about the letter to anyone.

Anyway, she thought smugly, *it's what everyone wants to happen. I'm just the only one brave enough to do anything about it,* Agatha reasoned within herself.

The weeks passed slowly until Pedro returned from his long travels to Cebu. When he arrived on the doorstep, Solidad ran up to meet him. She had missed her big brother and eagerly waited to see if he had brought her anything.

He looked bedraggled, a bit sunburned, and tired from the trip. His hair was tousled, and he needed a shave. But despite his weariness, he sat down with Solidad and fumbled around in his pack. With a smile, he pulled out the newest edition of an American fashion magazine, which he had brought back just for her.

"Maybe you'll find a few new haircuts in this one for me." He ran his dirty hands through his wild, windblown hair.

Solidad laughed and hugged the magazine to her chest. "Daghang salamat, manong Pedro. Thank you very much. Gusto ko` na! I like it!"

Pedro was happy to be home again. The windows were open, and light spilled across the wooded floor slats and brightened the leaves of the plants in terracotta pots, which were arranged on low shelves across from where he sat. The house looked clean, and the cheery sunshine warmed his unsettled heart.

Solidad and Antonia crouched together, and the sound of their voices filled the house like the sunbeams. Over and over again, Pedro could hear Antonia's soft laughter. When he crossed the room he could see them, the two heads, the sister and the friend, bent over the pictures in the magazine. He found a good many excuses for walking across the living room that afternoon.

At dinner that evening, the conversations centered on Pedro's trip to Cebu, as everyone was interested to hear what was going on in the second biggest city in the Philippines. Pedro was exhausted, but he found new strength surrounded by his loving family and their concern for his business. Strangely, Antonia was even quieter than she had been before he left.

"You all might be interested in the big news I heard while in Cebu. It seems that a certain woman pilot from America, named Amelia -- not Antonia," he smiled and continued, "took off to circumnavigate the earth along the equator in an airplane, but they lost contact with her plane at the beginning of July somewhere out over the Pacific ocean, just north of the equator.

She had planned to land on an uninhabited island far south of the Philippines, called Howland. From what they say, that island is just about as big as Suluan. I can show you where it is on my nautical map later. They are still looking for her or the remnants of her small aircraft. She was only 40 years old and was a very accomplished pilot and author. A very smart lady, I heard."

Solidad was concerned. "What a pity. Do you think she's out there afloat in the ocean?"

"No one knows for sure. She was an excellent pilot and was the first woman ever to cross the Atlantic solo in a plane. I heard on the radio that first Charles Lindbergh flew to France in 1927, and then Amelia followed with a co-pilot the next year. Then four years later, she did the flight alone.

This time, she attempted to do a much longer, more difficult flight. She had a navigator with her in the plane, who is also missing. And now, well... I guess she didn't make it.

She isn't used to water and boats like we are -- her method of travel is flying. They've looked for her for days, but I think I heard that they called off the search. Sad, no? What a tragedy to lose such a life at sea."

Antonia sat with her mouth open and her eyes moist and wide. She relived her fear of floating alone at sea -- being cold and scared -- encircled by hungry sharks.

"She must be very brave to have even wanted to fly an airplane. I pray someone finds her before... "

She stopped.

Thoughts of her own peril at sea were still too fresh in her memory.

"They called her 'Meelie' instead of Amelia. Amelia Earhart was her name." Pedro said softly.

Antonia sighed and scooted her chair closer to Solidad to grab her hand. She stared down at the floor as she spoke.

"Someday... I'd like to read a story about her."

Narciso, also visibly moved by the report, spoke with a solemn look on his face.

"It sounds like it's not just a man's world anymore, doesn't it? Imagine that, a young lady flew an airplane around the world. You girls are smart and brave and can do anything we men can do, it seems. Girls seem to have a special endurance for pain, more so than we men."

All the women at the table laughed.

"As a mother of four children, I can agree," Agatha said. "We can endure hardship, and we can even do it with a smile -- especially we Filipinas, di ba? Right, ladies?"

Even the men joined in the laughter after that remark.

The candles around the room grew small. Pilar said her good-byes and left with Agatha and Solidad to bring a few cups from the table to the kitchen on her way out the back door.

Peping and Quirino went with their father to the backyard to bring the chickens and ducks into their pens for the night. Pedro sat at the table a bit longer, tapped his fingers on the tabletop, and made small talk about the weather with Antonia as she readied her sofa with blankets for the night.

He saw her reach into a small box and pull out a piece of paper. She unfolded it, twisted her mouth, and gave him a quizzical and penetrating stare. Sitting down on the sofa, she cleared her throat, and he could tell she wanted to say something to him by the way she seemed to search for words.

He stopped drumming his fingers and waited for a full minute in silence before he finally spoke.

"Do you have something you'd like to tell me, Anod?"

"Um...well...I'm not sure what to say. I'm a bit confused about this... this note you left in my laundry before you sailed for Cebu."

"You found *what?*"

"And I, um… I thought that, well… I had assumed that you and Bibay were to be, um… *married* soon." She hesitated. "But now I… " she could not continue.

Again he waited in silence. Then, as he realized that she wasn't going to finish her sentence, he stood up and reached for the paper.

"May I see that, please?"

Antonia reluctantly handed him the paper, which by now she had read a hundred times, and looked down shyly at the floor again. Had he touched her arm, he would have felt the trembling in her body.

Pedro dropped his head in shock, and his eyes grew wide as he read the note. He felt embarrassed; his skin burned, and his face turned red and hot like a fire.

"Hmmm… this is not good," was all he managed to say in a very low tone. Stuffing the note in his pants pocket, he said, "Good-night, Anod. I guess I'll see you in the morning with everyone else at breakfast."

He turned and retreated to his room, blowing out the candle on the table as he walked past.

Antonia was embarrassed, too. Pedro had left so quickly that she never had the chance to see his face. Both had a restless night of sleep. Antonia was confused, and Pedro was furious.

However, Agatha and Pilar both fell asleep that night with smiles on their faces -- their dear Pedro was home, and they were both optimistic about the future. They did not expect that not everyone would find their schemes as appealing as they did.

Antonia was up before the rest of the family and managed to set the table and cook the rice without waking a soul. She went outside and sat on the front step. The breeze blew gently all around her.

Three chickens pecked at the dirt around her bare feet.

A group of children played with a scrawny dog on the road in front of the house. They all waved at Antonia.

Pedro appeared suddenly before her. He had come around from the backside of the house and had been looking for her. She looked up and felt the hot rush of embarrassment on her face.

"Anod, you need to know something. I did *not* write that letter," he said emphatically. "I didn't write it, and I didn't put it in your laundry. This is *crazy*. I have no idea what is going on here, but this is *not* a funny joke."

"Well, it looks like your handwriting... and it certainly is your signature. I found it in the pocket of my skirt right after you left. If you don't have feelings like this for me, then why did you write such words -- sharing your intentions so freely with me?"

"Really, Anod... I can imagine this is some trick of Peping. He likes to do things like this, you know. Believe me; it wasn't me. I'm still engaged to Bibay... and, well... I -- I am very sorry for this mix-up. This is very embarrassing."

"*Embarrassing?*" She closed her eyes. Her heart was beating loudly, and her hands trembled. "Yes, I think so, too."

She didn't look up at him.

"I'll see you later, Anod... I mean, Tonya."

He sprang to his feet. All at once Pedro's muscles tensed and a scowl spread across his face.

"Please excuse me from breakfast and tell my family that I won't be here today. I have work to do."

He spoke gruffly and vanished, then returned a few minutes later with his backpack slung over his shoulder and another small gray sack tucked under his left arm. As he left the yard, he didn't look back but headed straight for his ship with long, hard strides. He marched through town and did not stop to speak to anyone on his way.

Antonia sat stunned on the step.

Breakfast was awkward. Agatha and Pilar said very little after they heard that Pedro had left abruptly for his ship. Antonia looked as if she had been crying. The two women shot worried glances at each other while they ate. Even Solidad asked what was going on.

Narciso and the boys chatted about their fishing plans for the day with no inkling of the distress that lurked in the air around them. But they were about to find out.

An entire week passed, and neither word from nor sign came from Pedro. Then one mid-morning while she washed her clothes in the backyard, Antonia heard the muffled voices of Narciso, Agatha, and Pilar intensely discussing something.

That morning they had eaten another unnaturally quiet breakfast together. Something was not right. Half an hour had passed when Narciso finally emerged from the bedroom, a bit ruffled and very irate.

He fumed and called out the back door to tell Antonia that he was heading to the ship to find Pedro. She put down the wash and walked with him to the front of the house.

"Sus, Marie, Joseph!" he said tersely under his breath.

He marched out with the same strides that Antonia had witnessed a week before in Pedro's hurried gait.

Agatha appeared a minute later, and then came Pilar. The two sat nervously at the table and called Antonia in to join them. With shame and hesitation in their voices, the two confessed to their mischievous plot.

Antonia stifled a gasp. "And *you* signed Pedro's name to a love letter you wrote to *me*, Ate?"

Pilar nodded. Now she was the one who could not look Antonia in the eye.

"And he knew nothing of this -- and never asked you to do this for him? Antonia probed.

Pilar shook her head again.

"We just meant to help things out, dear one. But it looks as if we've made a few people very upset."

"Everyone can see how he cares for you," Agatha added.

Her face flushed.

Lowering her head, Antonia spoke again. "But... he's already promised to Bibay, and...who am I? I am so young, and he's so... so..." she stopped and took a breath. "I'm just an island girl -- a simple island girl -- and his Bibay, well...she's a real --" she paused.

"A real poor choice," continued Pilar. "Even he knows that. Haven't you seen how unhappy he is every time he comes home from a visit with her?"

"But Ate, they have made their plans, the wedding is set, and he loves her. What makes you so sure that..."

"*Does* he?"

Antonia shrugged her shoulders and nodded her head slowly. "Oo. Yes. She's his beautiful fiancée."

"Does he pick her up and twirl her around and laugh with her as he does with you, my child?"

Antonia bit her lip and made an embarrassing grimace. "He's like a brother to me. He would never... "

The two women were right. Pedro had never had a playful moment with Bibay as he had with Antonia. He gave Bibay no nickname, he didn't spend hours walking with her on the beach, he didn't bring her wild roses every week, and he didn't even talk much about her during meals. The family had noticed all these things. It dawned on Antonia also that perhaps Bibay was not the best choice for Pedro.

"He must be very embarrassed. And angry," said Antonia. "Maybe he won't ever talk with me again!"

Pilar stood up, smoothed down the front of her dress lightly with her hands, and went to peer out the front windows for a while to see if the men had returned from the dock. She turned around and looked back to the table.

"No, Antonia, he's much kinder than that. Moreover, he loves you. Maybe this was the right thing to do after all... to make him think about what he really wants. He still has time to choose what's best for him. I'm still convinced he just needed a little help from us."

"It is due to you," Pilar told her humbly. "He has never had a friend like you. And I see you -- how you've changed. It's like watching a flower open very slowly. From week to week I can hardly wait to see how it has opened since I saw you last."

Antonia smiled at her.

"Pedro is good for you," Pilar said, trying to choose her words carefully. "Would you not give him a chance to win your heart, my dear?"

A deep flush rose slowly from her throat to her temples. The momentary pleasure of the thought of being Pedro's girlfriend popped like a bubble on the waves. She was too far from home. She needed her family. All this was strange, and new, and different, and these emotions were so -- so unsure.

If she were honest with herself, she knew that she had feelings for Pedro -- and more than just as a big brother. She couldn't dare let Pilar or Agatha see the ray of hope that so obviously filled her countenance right then. She looked away, stood up, and made herself busy straightening her bed at the other end of the room.

The women decided together to carry on as if nothing had happened and hoped that this embarrassing situation would blow over. The men hadn't returned, so Pilar slipped out the front door and headed home. Agatha hoped that Pedro could forgive them for what they had

done, and she continued to believe he would soon come
to his senses and call off this ill-matched engagement to
Bibay.

In the heat of the morning hours, she went to work in
the kitchen and chopped mounds of fresh vegetables for
the soup she planned to make for lunch. She energetically
cut carrots, chayote, onions, garlic, ginger root, cabbage,
and bell peppers.

This domestic activity was a disguised outlet to vent
her frustration. Agatha fiercely hacked away at her cares
for much of the morning. She still also needed to catch,
kill, pluck, and cut up the chicken for the soup before
everyone returned for lunch.

Meanwhile, Antonia washed clothes in the backyard;
she sang quietly to cheer herself and keep her mind
focused on other things besides Pedro.

When the two men arrived an hour later, renewed
tension filled the air. They had brought it home with
them, but at least Pedro was with his family again.

Things continued around the house as if nothing had
happened. However, Antonia was acutely aware of
Pedro's every move, as he was of hers. Now the entire
family watched them closely.

A week passed before anyone broached the hot topic
of the love note in the laundry. In the meantime, Pedro
robotically fetched water for the family every morning as
usual and spoke very little to anyone as he went about his
chores.

Deep in his own thoughts, he no longer smiled, no
longer stayed up late to joke with his brothers, no longer
invited Antonia to go for long walks along the shoreline,
but rather went to bed early each night.

He left the house in the afternoons and returned
around dusk. Antonia and the family assumed that he was
going to call on Bibay. He did. As a surprise to everyone,

his visits became shorter and shorter. When he came home, he was always in a terrible mood, just as Pilar had said.

His temper worsened as the week passed. Pedro had difficulty sleeping. His previous weeks away in Cebu had not solved any of his problems, and all his time alone to think at sea brought him no answers. One thing was for sure: he felt trapped.

Narciso had seen, and felt, enough. On the following Saturday morning, he politely asked Antonia if the Sayson family could be alone to discuss something of a private matter. She smiled, nodded, and looked around the room for the new umbrella that Solidad had given to her as a gift.

Antonia gathered her belongings and headed out the door; she took a slow stroll up and down the narrow paths in the bustling village. She continued out to the shore and there found a scraggly rock upon which she climbed.

Although it was not the same rock where she had landed when she first arrived on Dinagat, it was similar in its size and color and brought back many memories of how she felt as she struggled to crawl out of the ocean, and how she spent her first night here on the island, naked, hungry and afraid.

To solve the family chaos, Narciso Sayson called an emergency family meeting, as he referred to it, and sat everyone down around the table to discuss the situation be-tween Pedro and Bibay. He did not call it an engagement any longer because he saw that Pedro was disengaged in his heart toward Bibay.

He was blunt and to the point, contrary both to his typical sensitive personality and to Philippine custom. Normally, Narciso followed the custom of circling around an issue for a time, the way a cat makes rings around a hot bowl of milk. However, the urgency of the "situation" demanded honesty and a large dose of tough love.

"Son, you know we love you, and that is exactly the reason why we need to be truthful with you this morning. It's about you and your relationship to Bibay. Pedro, I want to remind you that when you take a young lady as your bride, she marries not only you, but your entire family as well.

Therefore, because of that, I feel I need to remind you that the decision you have made to marry her affects all of us around this table, which includes your Ate Pilar."

Pedro set his jaw. The air was heavy with things still unsaid; questions crouched in the mind of every family member.

"Son, we want every happiness for you; of course we do. You are our eldest, our pride and joy, and a very important member of this family. We have all observed you the last months and have realized that rather than looking forward to and planning your wedding day with joy, as it should be, you are -- how should I say it... uh... dragging your feet."

His audience had listened in almost total silence. Only at the mention of the word 'joy' did Solidad draw a quick intake of breath and let out a frail cry which she quickly suppressed. Narciso shot a concerned glance at his only daughter, then looked quickly away and fixed his eyes on Pedro, who was frowning with intense concentration.

"And you are sad all the time, too," said Solidad. Her words came hurrying out. "You deserve a girl who will make you laugh!"

Narciso gave Solidad another stern look and put his finger over his lips. Apart from Narciso's glance at Solidad, none of them met one another's eyes.

"Pedro, we think it would be in the best interest for

you, for Bibay, and for all of the Sayson family, if you called off your wedding plans right away. We don't believe you need to think any more about it; you just need to go to Bibay and tell her that you are sorry. Perhaps it would be best if your momma and I went with you and we met with the parents of Bibay, too."

Pedro shot up straight and banged his fist on the table.

"What is this?! Are you all telling me who I can marry -- and who I cannot? Aren't I old enough to make those decisions for myself? This is not fair to me, nor is it fair to Bibay. What will everyone think if I cancel our plans now?"

"Is that what you are afraid of, Pedro?" asked his mother. "What other people will think? Son, this is your life -- the rest of your life -- and you will have to live with your decision from that day on until forever."

He sat down and was silent. Everyone sat still and waited to see who would speak next. Pilar was afraid that Narciso had hurt Pedro's feelings and was feeling pity for him.

"Pedro," she spoke up, "as your Ate, you know I want your complete happiness. Can you ever forgive me that I wrote the note to Tonya and signed your name to it? I'm very sorry."

As he remembered the note, he felt hot flashes of embarrassment. He looked away and clucked his tongue in disgust.

How could she do that to me?

"I'm sorry I got so angry with everyone. It's just that this whole thing with Bibay has made me so confused. She really is a wonderful girl. Maybe if I just give it a bit of time... "

Narciso did not even let him finish his sentence. "No, Pedro! This has gone on long enough, and we don't think it is fair to Bibay, let alone to you. Please consider what we are all trying to say to you this morning. Please call off your engagement to Bibay."

Pedro stood slowly, looked around the table, and thanked his family. Dogs were barking loudly outside, but around the table all had grown silent. Their words closed in on his own secret doubts. He turned away and ducked through the open doorway.

After he left the house, no one knew if his brief mumbled "thank you" was heartfelt or obligatory. Peping and Quirino, sat quietly. No one moved a muscle. The two had never seen their oldest brother so troubled before, and they didn't know whether to give him their allegiance or trust the wisdom of their elders. Rather than say another word, they held their opinions to themselves.

Solidad sat and cried silently. Pilar and Agatha praised Narciso for his courage and skill in communicating his views.

What would Pedro do? Did he really hear what his father had told him? Would he marry Bibay in spite of all sound counsel from those who knew and loved him best?

CHAPTER EIGHTEEN
THE DISCOVERY

Early the next morning, Pedro had his bags packed and waiting for him at the front door. He had decided not to stay for breakfast with his family, since he needed to set sail quickly in order to deliver the next shipment of mangrove wood to four new customers in Cebu. He would be back as soon as he could, he said.

He had not mentioned anything about what his plans were regarding Bibay, but Pilar could sense that she had been forgiven. Everyone was a bit melancholy to see him leave so soon again, especially Solidad. She was worried about her manong Pedro, her oldest brother.

Weeks later, they would find out why his boat did not leave for another two hours.

After a hearty breakfast, the family dispersed, each going his or her own separate way with this or that chore or activity for the day. Since she was now able to walk and her strength had returned, Antonia cleaned the house for Agatha each morning. After she swept the sala, the living area, she dusted the furniture and wiped down the wooden tabletops. Then she made her way into the bedrooms.

She loved looking at all the odds and ends in Pedro's room. The collections of large conch seashells, the beautiful blue starfish, and the array of maritime gadgets in his room all showed Antonia Pedro's great love for the sea. What a contrast to her own gnawing fear of ever having to sail again. His room looked to her how she imagined a museum would be.

Antonia lingered as she slowly straightened his piles of paperwork at his desk and meticulously swept the floor. She chased a few large spiders with her broom and frightened a thin brownish gecko lizard that had been hiding in a corner.

A candle rested on a rickety square table next to the single bed. Above his bed was a wooden shelf with a half-dozen books. Three fishing rods, a spear, and a net in need of repair leaned against the wall to the right of the window.

A pair of beige pants loosely hung on a wooden post next to his bed. A small piece of paper with her name scribbled on it peered out from the top of the pants pocket. Without hesitation, she took the note and sat on the bed to unfold it.

She thought about what Pedro would think if he entered the room right now. Antonia's hands trembled. Her name was on the paper, and so she thought: This must be for me to read.

She smiled. The endearing words in this letter made the former note, written by Ate Pilar, pale in comparison. She sat breathless on the bedside.

Pedro had filled the page with his most loving concern for Antonia's welfare. He poured out his heart and told her that because of her coming to their island and into their home -- and most of all, into his life -- he had become a better man.

The further she read the more convinced she became that Pedro was truly in love with her. He did not want to marry Bibay, nor did he love his fiancé; he made that very clear. He said that he only had eyes for her, and for her alone. He finished the note with the promise that he would hurry home to speak with her face to face.

Antonia's legs went numb. Her fifteen-year-old heart beat wildly, and her hands still shook. She sat still and lost track of time. Then, she began to wonder.

What if this was just another foolish match-making attempt from someone else in the family? Would they do such a thing again to Pedro... and to me?

She folded the note up neatly and tucked it deep within her skirt pocket, holding her smile far behind her furrowed brow and pursed lips.

Then she found something that would change her mind and cause her to doubt her doubts and trust her heart. It happened later that morning as she brought in the laundry that had hung dry in the yard. She saw yet another piece of paper with her name on it that stuck out of a shirt pocket that belonged to Pedro.

She was sure it was his shirt -- the dark blue one he wore when he returned from Cebu last week. With trembling hands, she removed the paper and read:

My ever dearest Anod, I'm hoping you will find all of the notes I've hidden around the house today. By the time I return with gifts for you from Cebu, I hope that you will be convinced that you are truly the love of my life. Destiny brought you from Suluan to the shores of my heart. My sincere hope and most fervent prayer is that you also feel as I do. As of today, there will no longer be a wedding with Bibay. She is not the girl of my dreams... you are!

Antonia felt the blood drain from her head. She was dizzy and had to sit down on the rickety stool near the dirty kitchen. The piles of stiff laundry on her lap comforted her as she found the blue shirt of Pedro and held it to her chest.

Then she buried her face in it and breathed in the fresh smell of sunshine and of Pedro. Tonya's heart melted at the thought of Pedro's attraction to her.

"He loves me? *He loves me.* Yes, he wrote it. He wrote

this note," she whispered the words aloud over and over to herself.

She paused in her thoughts, embarrassed. Then her face broke into a smile. Her dark eyes glistened with tears of joy. Their love had begun quietly, yet it now seemed to shout within her heart.

The chasm of loss in which she had found herself closed. Now she stood on top of the abyss -- she was finally out of the pit. This love rescued her. Miraculously, Antonia's whole being somehow, in some way, was filled with peace!

For the rest of the morning, Antonia went on a treasure hunt. She sought the tiny slips of paper that Pedro had cleverly hidden in strange nooks and crannies throughout the house and out in the garden. She had thoroughly cleaned the house this morning, but had overlooked half a dozen notes which he had skillfully tucked into inconspicuous places.

One note was wedged between the bananas on a kitchen shelf, one inside the burlap bag of rice in the corner. One she found under her blanket where she'd slept. Another lay among the flowers along the side of the house. She found three more notes tucked in his laundry.

His tender sentiments overwhelmed her. Luckily no one else was home as she searched high and low for more hidden love notes with her name on them.

"I'm home!" Pedro called as he lumbered through the front door with a smile, his luggage, and a host of packages.

Weeks had passed since he had stormed out of the house and left for Cebu City. He looked like a new man. His face was freshly bronzed by the sun. His hair was neatly cut, washed, and combed to the side. He had even bought himself a new polo shirt.

Pedro brought strength with him as he bounded into the living room. From every corner came his family, everyone glad and relieved to see him home again not the least, Antonia, who stood quickly when he entered the door. A sudden tightness twisted in her chest. No one had expected him to land today.

"Pedro, my son, I'm so happy you are home again!" His father gave him a slap on the back and grabbed one of his son's heavy bags to relieve his load.

Solidad ran in from the dirty kitchen outside, where she had been cooking. In her haste, she forgot to put down her wooden spoon, caked and dripping with rice. She appeared in a grimy apron tied loosely around her waist.

"Oh, my big brother has finally returned from his travels! I missed you so, kuya! I don't like it when you are gone!"

Pedro lifted his sister up and twirled her around. Her wooden spoon filled with sticky rice fell to the floor and bounced under the table.

"And... kuya... anything for me in all these bags? Perhaps a new fashion magazine from Cebu maybe?"

He smiled warmly and nodded as he set her on her feet. Solidad kissed him on the cheek and clapped her hands.

"Oh, daghang salamat! Thank you so much!" she said.

"Ma! Good to see you, Ma!" Pedro greeted Agatha with a gentle but strong hug. "Ma, kumusta, Ma? How are you? I missed my one and only mama. Cebu is too far away from your good cooking!"

"Oh, my boy. It's good you're safely home. Come, sit down and take your rest. We'll have dinner soon. I hope you're hungry -- and that you brought some fish with you!" she said.

"Oo, yes, Ma," he said raising his eyebrows quickly, "I gave Peping my catch at the dock, and he and Quirino are out back with the huge tuna I caught. They'll have it cleaned and ready to grill in no time. Tonight we're going to have a feast. We have a lot to celebrate!"

He laughed and turned toward Antonia, who hadn't moved an inch since she saw him.

"Now... where is my girl?"

His auntie Pilar had entered a moment before and stood with baited breath at the side of the big wooden dining table. She watched as Pedro walked without hesitation over to Antonia and said hello. Antonia put her hand over her mouth and laughed, but tears had sprung into her eyes. She didn't know where to look and didn't know what to say.

"Ayaw kaguol. Magmalipayon ka. Don't be sad. Be happy," Pedro said to her. He turned around and said to his family, "I want to marry this beautiful maiden from the sea." Then he turned to her, stretched out his hands and said, "That is, if she will have me. What do you say, Anod? Will you marry me?"

Antonia was silent for a moment. "I... I... I think you will have to ask permission from my papa back home on Suluan. But as for me... " She stood shocked. "I would be the happiest girl on earth if I were to be your wife, Pedro."

Antonia's silver laugher tinkled in the quiet room. Pilar hesitated, and then spoke up from across the room.

"I think this would make us the luckiest family in the Philippines! Now I know why this shark brought you through the storm to our shores, my dear. Our Pedro needed a very special wife. You are an 'import' from far away."

Antonia's forehead wrinkled in an effort to put her thoughts into words.

"I never thought of it that way," she said, her eyes clouding. "Is that why, do you think, the shark knew to come exactly to *this* island and not to another shore?"

Everyone laughed and encircled the two. Peping and Quirino came in from the backyard as they heard the news.

"Hey, little sister," said Peping. "You need to ask this sailor if he'll take you home to meet your parents." He made a fist, boxed his brother on the shoulder, and clucked his tongue.

Quirino added, "Maybe I can join you. I hear there are a lot of pretty girls on Suluan. Maybe I'll be fortunate like my big brother here. Do girls wash ashore there, too?"

"Okay, okay. When do we set sail, boys?" Pedro looked at his two brothers. "I say, the sooner, the better. Is this fine with you, Dad?"

"Well, there is still one question that concerns me, son." He cleared his throat and spoke softly. "What about your proposal to Bibay?" Narciso looked steadily into the narrowed black eyes of Pedro.

A hush fell in the room. Solidad walked over to Antonia and put an arm around her waist. They all looked to Pedro for his answer. Antonia held her breath. He began to explain.

"Two weeks ago, on the day I left, I spent a couple of hours with Bibay and her family. It wasn't easy, I can tell you that. I know I hurt them. I especially disappointed Bibay. I don't think she'll ever speak to me again. But I know I made the right decision. Ate Pilar, I know I have you and your silly match-making to thank for this."

Pilar winked and blew him a kiss.

"Yes. I think sometimes loves needs a little push in the right direction. In your case, you certainly needed a shove!"

"Oo. Yes. And a very romantic love letter stuffed in

some laundry," said Solidad.

Pedro laughed again. He turned to Antonia.

"You wanna go walk on the shore before we eat?"

It wasn't yet dark. Solidad came along but followed ten steps behind them. They walked out to the beach in silence, Pedro accommodating his long strides with Antonia's less certain steps.

The tide was retreating as they strolled down to the strip of damp sand at the edge of the curling waves, climbing over several larger rocks. Numerous pastel seashells were imbedded underfoot in the sand, and clumps of soggy seaweed lined the shoreline.

They had walked about two hundred yards when Pedro said quietly, "So Anod, what is in your heart? What are your thoughts right now?"

Antonia looked out to sea and studied the horizon as she weighed her words carefully. Pedro stopped walking, turned towards her, and folded his arms high across his broad chest.

Along the frame of the beach a fringe of long grasses blew in the gently-moving moist air of late afternoon.

"You know," she started hesitantly, "I have felt so at home here. So at home with you, Pedro; You, your family -- you all have done more for me than I can ever repay you for. You have treated me like your own kin. I was a stranger, and you took me in. You fed me, clothed me, and taught me to walk again. Because of you, I found my voice. I'm finding healing. I am finding my purpose. Each of you had a part to play in my recovery."

"Yeah, there's nothing like finding a mermaid washed ashore to bring a family together, is there?" he said.

He took her small hand in his. She shivered and stared down at her bare feet on the sand.

"I'm still amazed that I survived. You saved my life."

"You coming opened my eyes up to life."

"*Really*, Pedro?"

"My mom tells me over and over that we were all created for a different kind of world. I believe her. You coming to us, living through your pain with you, seeing you fight to find your way back to life, well it showed me how fragile life here on earth is. I believe our Creator has a much higher plan for all of us... both now and also with Him in heaven someday.

But now, I realize that He wants me -- *us* -- to get as much out of life as we can. I don't want to settle for just limping along in life. I've come to love this kind of life that I have when I am with you."

"But why did you break off your engagement to Bibay? She is so lovely, so perfect. She's strong and smart... isn't life with her the kind of life you want? I mean, after all, she is so, uh, so *grown-up*."

She stood in uncertain silence.

"Anod, Bibay was a bit of a shark. I have great respect for her, or maybe it was more like fear. I don't know. But her ways are not tender, like yours are. Oh, how can I explain it to you? She was like a typhoon in my life. She pushed me around. Often I felt like I was drowning when I was with her. I never knew where I was or if I was safe. It was clear to me the more I was around you."

Pedro pulled Antonia close to his side. His breath warmed her forehead. She could feel that he was strong and safe. He lifted her up and twirled her around, and her legs flew through the air as they spun in circles together.

He really does love me, she thought.

Antonia let out her breath. "All this --" she exclaimed, the sweep of her arm including the deepening blue of the sky, the shining ocean in the distance, and the myriad of sea shells lining the shoreline. "How beautiful!" She sighed. "There is just -- just so much; so many happy things. It is beautiful just to be alive in your world -- on your island!"

Antonia's smile was bright and wide and finally free. She was aware all at once of Pedro watching her, and their hands joined. A red blush surged up into her smooth cheeks. For a moment, neither of them moved.

"Look!" she whispered.

He followed her gaze back down the sandy beach to a lone figure silhouetted against the sky.

Solidad sat on a rock in the distance, her gaze fixed on the in-and-out surge of the clear water below her. The red ball of sun sank into the sea, and its beautiful reflection bounced in on every little ripple. As the light faded to the color of twilight, the sound of the sea intensified, its soft rhythmic moaning rising to a softened roar.

The shouts and the laughter of the children playing behind her on the shore slowly silenced as they all ran home for dinner. She tried not to pay attention to her brother and Antonia, but she had heard their laughter and Antonia's screams.

"There's going to be a wedding soon," she said to the sea.

With a satisfying smile, she looked up toward the couple and waved for them to come.

The last light of day spread itself in gray tones over the great waste of sea. A fine drizzle fell, and the air tasted sweet. It was time to head back to the house. Time to return to this place called Suluan.

CHAPTER NINETEEN
THE HOMECOMING

A halo of summer sunshine wrapped around Antonia's head. Overhead, barely discernible against the blue of the sky, a long gray shadow hung suspended. Several clouds had blown into the otherwise perfect day. Below her, wave upon wave crashed against the side of the big boat in explosions of spray, shooting orbs of spume dancing and rolling like iridescent bubbles on the ridges of the water encircling them.

Antonia felt secure standing at Pedro's side as he captained the vessel. But as soon as she walked away, anxiety gripped at her heart. The wind blew strong and the booming of the boat reminded Antonia of her last time upon the sea.

As they sailed toward her home, a stretch of turbulent sea, white-specked with whitecaps to the horizon, lay before her. She ignored the sky that teased her fears with its mocking shadows of darkness behind few clouds.

Pedro's large family sailboat was packed full with almost one hundred people from Dinagat. Everyone wanted to make the trip to Suluan to bring Antonia back to her home place. This was a major event for the entire village.

"I can only imagine how everyone will be surprised when they see me again," she said, barely loud enough for Pedro to hear. "I know they thought I'd died with the others." She paused and found it hard to swallow. "Pedro, what do you think? Do you believe that any of the boys made it back home?"

Pedro shook his head. "Anod, we'll see. From what you've told me, that was a strong storm -- and the boys had a long, long way to swim to get back to shore. We'll see," he said. "We'll see."

How changed she was, he thought, his heart filled with hope as he gazed at Antonia.

Her stay on Dinagat Island had opened for her a whole new world. His young "Anod" was more confident, more secure in herself. She had learned to walk and to talk; like a newborn child, she spent the last months discovering the world around her with a positive outlook.

Something about her young face fascinated him -- a searching and a wistfulness that struck him. Perhaps it was only his imagining. Nonetheless, it stirred in him a yearning for her that he could not put into words.

The two stood together, staring out across the sea. They stood silent for a long time, and then Pedro asked, very carefully, "If your father is home today, do you think he will welcome me?"

A sheepish grin spread across Antonia's face as she drew in her breath. She looked up at his dark brown face and nodded. Quickly, she looked back out to the sea and cupped her hand over her smile. After a minute, she spoke.

"Why? Are you worried that he might think you kidnapped me? Or that you've come to take me away?" she spoke out toward the sea as if she were questioning the fish swimming below.

"Well. Actually... yes. I want to take you away, Anod. I want to ask if I can have your hand in marriage. I want to take you back with me to Dinagat -- that is, if he will let you go -- again. And, if you will have me."

He clapped his hands together and peered down sheepishly at her. Their eyes met. Antonia raised her eyebrows a few times and scrunched her nose with a look of uncertainty.

"I honestly don't know what to think, Pedro. They will be shocked. I just don't know."

"You don't know about your decision?" he asked. "Will *you* have me? Will you be my wife?"

Antonia let out a laugh that the sea breeze caught and blew in all directions. She tightened her grip on the rail of the ship and threw her head back. It felt good to be so happy again.

The ship approached an island of many palms and reddish clay, and Antonia explained that this was Homonhon, which neighbored Suluan. Her history lessons from school came in handy as Pedro's brothers and a group of about twenty five men encircled Antonia and pounded her with questions.

She recalled gruesome stories about Magellan and his three Spanish ships that sailed a perilous four-month voyage, during which they saw no land and had no chance to make fresh provisions.

Antonia remembered reading excerpts from their travel diaries that detailed how they ate biscuits which were no longer biscuits, but only powder, for the food was swarming with worms.

Everything stank strongly from the urine of rats. The men had to drink putrefied yellow water and often ate sawdust from boards of old wood. Above all misfortunes, the gums of both lower and upper teeth of some men swelled so that they could not eat and therefore died.

The men around Antonia groaned at the thought of

such suffering at sea. But she continued. This was important local history -- and, after all, she had suffered at sea as well.

At dawn on March 16, the Spanish explorers came upon the island of Homonhon. While still anchored, several canoes carrying the chiefs of Suluan and their datu chieftain, Garas-Garas, visited Magellan.

They boarded the ship, and Magellan explained to them through his interpreter, Enrique, that their King in Spain had sent them to spread the faith of Christ and convert these new friends to the true religion.

So the weary Spaniards disembarked and pitched their tents, and those suffering from scurvy recovered by eating coconuts and other fruits and vegetables. Meanwhile, Garas-Garas caught a great quantity of fish and provided the party of Magellan with food. As they were so well received, they called Homonhon, Nueva Providencia.

The following day, Garas-Garas presented his gifts to Magellan: two large jars of rice, a bamboo tube full of honey, pigs, fowl, fruits, vegetables such as eggplants, and a gold-headed baton. Magellan refused the baton, saying that it was of too much value.

He gave Garas-Garas a pearly-colored cloak of wool, a purple hat, several shirts of merino wool, Toledo knives, mirrors, and silver buttons. Garas-Garas divided the gifts among his people and brought out a jar of tuba (wine made from coconut tree sap) so they could drink to each other's health.

They agreed to celebrate a treaty of friendship. Then, they celebrated the island's first Roman Catholic mass and raised a tall cross near the shore.

Antonia amazed herself with how much history she remembered. The closer the ship came into familiar waters, the livelier and more talkative she became. Her stomach felt nervous, and her thoughts raced like fish darting every which way under choppy waters.

Under the deck, she saw the same swirling currents that had once pulled her out to sea. These enemies had forcibly dragged her away from home and her friends. She rode on top of them now in Pedro's big sailboat, unaffected and secure.

But her legs shook uncontrollably as they rebelled against her will. As the ship passed to the right of Homonhon, she caught sight of her beloved Suluan. Her heart beat faster seeing the view of its long shape, silhouetted against a deep blue sky in the distance.

Antonia's body quivered. Soon, she caught a glimpse of the lighthouse perched high above the cliffs on the far eastern side of the island.

"There's our lighthouse, Pedro!" she cried out, jumping up onto her toes and pointing to the east end of Suluan.

Remember I told you all about that place. I've got to take you there. And those -- those up there are the cliffs. That's where Bevs and I used to go when we were home from school on vacation. And... that was the last place we all gathered before we left for the wedding. Those cliffs are... *dangerous*!"

Her voice faded.

Antonia nervously paced back and forth across the deck. She pulled at her still-short, scruffy head of hair and tugged at the twisted shark's tooth necklace she wore around her neck.

Pedro paced the ship with a swaggering step and a wide grin. His face was alive. His shoulders pulled back with pride and confidence.

"My heart is smiling so hard. And yet I'm nervous and sad, and I'm about to cry," Antonia said.

"Have you thought about what you will say about me

to your parents, Tonya?"

"Oh, I've rehearsed it a million times, but I just don't know what they will think. I wonder if they will understand. I wonder if they will allow me. "

She looked up and saw three familiar figures. As the boat drew nearer to shore, she recognized them as old friends. She was coming home.

The anchor dropped, and the men pushed a long plank out to the beach. A short walk across the outstretched wooden board and there she was -- returned to her home. Antonia stood still and alone at the edge of Suluan's sandy shoreline.

Papa Beni, Mam Salud, and Osting stood afar off in shadows of gray haze and grief under a group of tall palms. At once, Antonia felt great pity for them. Beni stood on the wet sand, a sturdy, barefoot fisherman clothed in a familiar rough cotton shirt, rolled up haphazardly at the sleeves. His exposed lower arms hung limp, bare, and blackened by the years of hard work at sea and on his farm, his face etched deep with grooves of worry.

His wife, Salud, still rotund and full of face, stood with drooped shoulders. A half-scowl marred her normally cheerful countenance. Squinting, Salud shielded her eyes as she tried to make out the big ship that had landed on her island.

Antonia could not imagine what their lives had been like the last six months. Peter's father, Osting, looked fragile, aged and weakened from months of prolonged heartache. Anguish remained in his soul from the torture of watching his only son die a slow, feverish death.

Memories of Peter struggling with the rudder during the storm flashed before her eyes. Perhaps Osting also carried a burden of guilt that he had allowed his son to man the sailboat that had taken the teens into the storm.

Sorrow grabbed at her throat. Just the thought of voicing her regret to these parents was almost too much to bear. She was suddenly afraid of the pain that remained deep in her soul. Death overshadowed the entire island; a mist of misery hung heavy in the humid air.

And what Pedro had said to her before they landed was right; the parents would always carry a sense of guilt and shame. The mental picture of the boys, struggling to swim home in the middle of the typhoon rain, remained a bur in her mind, not easily shaken off, even after all these months on Dinagat.

Antonia found it hard to breath. Her skin prickled. She stood with clenched fists and began to sway. Her toes wiggled deep into the wet sand for support.

Living another day without her friends, without her dearest Bevs, was unthinkable. But here she was, somehow in the midst of yet another day. Life was moving forward, like the tide that freely splashed onto the shore at her back.

Today, returning to the place of beginnings, Antonia started over at age fifteen. A new life had begun; she was a new girl. The waves and wind blew behind her like howling trumpets. Were they trumpets of victory that she survived and now stood on the shores of Suluan, or rather a dirge of aching remorse?

Here I am, still alive and well.

She hung her head and began to weep aloud.

Salud was the first to recognize Antonia as she peered out into the glaring sun from within the shadows. Outlined with light, this frail, dark-skinned teen with cropped straggly hair was their Tonya! Salud grabbed Papa Beni by the hand, digging her short nails into his leathery skin, and shouted to Osting.

198

"It's our Antonia! It's *Tonya...* don't you see her there? She has returned to Suluan! She's alive; she's really alive. She's back. Our girl is home!"

The dismal spirit of grief choking the elders on the beach broke like a bolt of lightning splitting the sky as they stumbled through the sand toward Antonia. The commotion at the water's edge alerted others gathered not far from the shoreline. In an instant, the beach was full of old familiar faces, all screaming, laughing, and crying, pulling at Antonia's arms and kissing her cheeks, now soaked with tears.

Then some strong man lifted her up on his shoulders and cried out, "Let's bring this young girl back to her parents! Come on, they won't believe it. Our Tonya is alive! She's alive! She's alive!" he shouted.

Cheers broke out, followed by more clapping. The little children all squealed and jumped up, trying to reach Antonia's skirt and pull on her. Pedro and the crew from Dinagat followed close behind the throng, heading up the beach. Antonia's head flew backwards as she laughed and cried at the same time.

This was how she landed before her small home; the crowd of well-wishers waited in hushed stillness outside the door as Antonia slowly entered to find her father seated at their wooden dining table. Her eyes grew wide, and her throat felt as if she had swallowed a mango whole. She paused under the door frame.

Antonia's father, Bonifacio, blinked hard, as if he did not recognize his own daughter when he saw her for the first time. Then his face lit up with a tender smile. He was wearing his favorite old blue tee-shirt that Antonia remembered well.

Standing slowly, he opened his arms wide as Antonia

ran into his embrace. She buried her head in his chest and breathed in the smell of her fisherman father. Sweat, sunshine, saltwater, fish blood -- this was her papa! His hug tightened as he relished the touch of his little girl whom he had feared to be dead. She was finally home.

"I have never stopped believing, Tonya. You know that -- never!"

Bonifacio's voice shook with earnestness. His eyes glistened in the morning light and fixed penetratingly on his daughter's face. The two stood in a long embrace in the narrow hallway of their home.

Antonia took a step back and lifted her father's right hand to her bowed forehead. He stared at his girl and wiped his face with his free hand.

The ten-hour trip from Dinagat back to Suluan that had led to this moment with her beloved father had been an adventure for Antonia. Bonifacio did not move for a full minute, standing erect but motionless, pausing to recover from his shock. He took a deep breath, and pulled Antonia into the living area and sat her down while he disappeared.

Before he had a chance to dash up the stairs to find Macaria, she came bounding down the steps, two at a time, with a shout that sounded more like a painful scream.

Antonia's mother had awakened to the confusion and yelling in the village and, as if in a dream, rose slowly when she heard her daughter's voice in her own living room downstairs.

"My girl," Macaria said as she held her daughter's head hard against her chest. "You're... you're... alive! You've come home to us. Salamat sa Ginoo! Salamat sa Ginoo! Thank the Lord!"

Antonia could feel her mother's heart beating wildly as hot tears dropped onto her shoulder. Then all at once, her mother's knees buckled, and Macaria slowly sank to the wooden slatted floor. The fears, bitterness, and anger stored up within her soul these many months had taken their toll. She collapsed in a heap of pain and suffering at Antonia's bare feet.

Antonia bent down to cradle her head in her hands, and then she glanced up for help. Bonifacio squatted low to scoop up his frail wife in his large hands and then brought her over to the rattan bench at the end of the room and set her down gently.

His massive body frame hovered over his now unconscious wife. When she finally came to, Macaria simply smiled at Antonia. She was shaking.

"How did you survive, my Tonya? We thought you had died, like all the others. How did you find your way back to us?" Macaria asked.

"You mean none of the boys made it home, Mama?" Antonia asked. Her throat turned dry again. "Not even manong Carlo?" Not even my dear Carlo.

Macaria rocked her head back and forth as tears welled up in her eyes. Bonifacio put his arm around his daughter's shaking shoulders, and the three of them remained quiet. After a few minutes he began to speak, haltingly at first, but then with firmness in his voice.

Antonia braced herself. *If only this were a dream.*

"Tonya, all the boys are heroes. None of them lived, but they were the bravest sailors we've known. They did their best to save you girls. All of them are gone, my girl. All of them, even our Carlo."

"No, Papa... " Antonia said.

"Jhun, Rey, Peter, and Alfredo made it back to Suluan with Carlo. But the boys all suffered; they endured the terrible storm and had a long fight back through cold waters without any food or drink. By the time they arrived, they were full of fever and half-crazed with fear.

We did our best to save them, but one by one, they each passed away."

"And the others?" Antonia asked.

"Domingo, Roger, and Mario didn't make it to the shore at all. The storm was just too strong, Tonya. We men went out looking for them and for you girls, but with no luck. We feared the worse -- and knew of the currents, and the shark. All we found were pieces of Osting's sailboat here and there. We've since found no bodies."

"Oh Papa, how terrible," said Antonia. She buried her face in her hands and cried.

"Anak, my child, what about the girls? Are you the only one who returned today?" asked Bonifacio.

Antonia nodded and a shiver ran through her body.

"Oo, yes Pa, I'm the only one left."

Antonia explained the details of each friend's struggle, as the faces of her parents grew grim. Heaviness filled the room like the clouds before a storm. Any flicker of hope immediately vanished. Macaria grasped her daughter's hand tightly and held it close to her lips.

She would never again let her go. She knew the sea was a dangerous place; her years of worry had proven her right. What she greatly feared had come upon her. Macaria glanced up at Bonifacio, scowled, and shook her head. But Bonifacio calmly smiled.

"Sweetheart," he said, "our girl is a survivor. I knew the good Lord would bring her home to us. At least I had that small hope."

He pulled Antonia close to his broad chest and squeezed her.

"Tonya – how did you make it back to us? Tell us the miracle."

Antonia explained about her escapades with Bevs up to the cave and the cliffs; she told of the despidita party for Carlo and Daisy with her friends the day before they

202

left for Guiuan, and of the suspicious dark cloud; she told about the typhoon, which shattered not only Osting's sailboat, but the lives of her best friends.

Her island innocence also sank into the sea along with the death of her five girlfriends. As Antonia shared of the currents, her struggles under the scorching sun by day and the frightful black waters by night, she shivered uncontrollably.

"Waves pulled me forward, tearing at me and dragging me away from everything I loved. Just thinking of you both, of my home on Suluan... that helped me stay alive," she said.

Then a slow smile spread across her face and a sparkle appeared in her dark eyes.

"Mama, Papa, you won't believe it. Something happened that I can't explain. I know it was a miracle; really, a miracle!"

Macaria stared in numb confusion.

"Well, what was it? Heaven knows we were all praying for you," she said. "Did God send an angel? A fisherman?"

Macaria swung her legs down off of the sofa and sat erect, full of anticipation.

Antonia sat down close to her mama on the wooden slats and grabbed her hands within her own.

"Ma, you won't believe it! I don't know exactly how to explain it," she began. Antonia stumbled over her words. "It was as if -- as if he spoke to me. He was the biggest, the strongest, and he scared all the other sharks away from me! He even glowed in the dark."

"Sharks? *What?!* What was it? What do you mean, 'he glowed'?" Macaria asked. Her questions tumbled out.

Antonia stood up and paced the floor.

"It was an ihutiki, a whale shark, Mama! Isdantuko in Tagalog, tawiki in Bisayan -- the language of the people on the island where I landed; that's what they call him. It was like he spoke to me and wanted to help me. I rode him! It was like he knew I was dying and he slowly carried me on his back, above the water.

I was so scared, but I hung on to his big fin and closed my eyes as he carried me. Ihutiki brought me to another people on an island called Dinagat. That big shark saved my life!"

Antonia told details of her miraculous ride and how the gargantuan whale shark gently dropped her in the shallow waters of Dinagat Island. Her account of the Sayson family's care for her brought with it a flood of mixed emotions.

The nights of horror, when she would awaken herself with a shout, were best left out of her story. So, too, the weeks of darkness and depression, the fear and the loneliness, and the tormenting guilt she battled like the non-stop pounding surf during a storm. She focused rather, on the good.

CHAPTER TWENTY
THE WEDDING

Pedro's head peeked out above the growing crowd of people standing in front of the Arceno's home. Careful not to disturb the reunion he witnessed through the open door, he was in no hurry to make himself known. So he waited.

Mixed feelings washed over him. There was something soothing and sacred about watching his lovely Antonia release her tears and grief into the supportive love of her parents. All around him relatives and neighbors clamored to get a glimpse of Antonia.

They knew nothing of her trauma and guilt; the dissonance of chatter and laughter outside rose like a note out of place in a melodic song. He cast his eyes to the ground and wished that he could run into the room and ease everyone's pain.

Lifting his head, his eyes met Antonia's and she offered him a weak smile and nodded. This was his sign to enter. Pedro hardly breathed while staring at her, pushing himself through the throng to get inside.

Will I know what to say? Is it wise to break into this holy moment of reunion and suffering? he asked himself.

Antonia's parents looked up as they heard footsteps entering the room. Some of the frown wrinkles left Bonifacio's face and he smiled as the stranger came near. That was a good sign. Pedro reached out his hand out to shake his.

"I'm Pedro Sayson from Dinagat Island, sir. Please to meet you. You must be Tonya's parents. I've heard so much about you both, and about Suluan."

The music of Pedro's kind words of introduction wound in and out of the corners of the small house and filled Antonia's whole world with healing. Her eyes sparkled with her new-found joy. Love, hurt and hope wrapped together within her like a thickly braided cord.

Antonia's struggles: the loneliness of being separated from Suluan, and her deep desire to be reunited with her family, began to fade. She felt swept away on an ocean current of happiness. How she wished to speak as clearly as Pedro, but Antonia was speechless. Numbly, she sat down next to her mother and let the melody of his voice wash over her.

How and when was Pedro going to talk to her parents about his hope to marry her? Would her parents say yes? Would they allow her to leave Suluan?

In bed that night, Antonia pondered her and Pedro's plans to marry. She pictured herself breathlessly twirling in a gown of white and lace. Surprisingly, her Papa had easily agreed to Pedro's proposal and said he would give the hand of his daughter in marriage to this young man from Dinagat.

Macaria was delighted. However, her euphoria was short-lived as soon as she realized that this young man from Dinagat Island would take her daughter away again. With that revelation, she fell moaning upon Antonia's neck and wept.

Pulling the thin blanket up to her chin, Antonia blinked back tears of joy. She listened to the constant noise outside her bedroom window: the crowing of a rooster, the barking of a dog, and waves hitting the shore; they all clamored for her attention.

Nothing tonight had the power to distract her vivid imagination of becoming Mrs. Pedro Sayson. Antonia slept a satisfying sleep in her own slatted wood-framed bed and dreamt of the cave and the high cliffs of Suluan.

Dawn was still painting the east in rosy colors when she tip-toed out of bed and walked down to the shoreline behind her house. The coolness of the early morning met Antonia, before the sun brought its heat upon the day.

Her bare feet were wet and full with sand as she dug her toes into the familiar beach. Antonia thought back to the last time she stood on this beach the night before they sailed for Guiuan. The earth beneath her seemed to drop away, leaving her hanging in space.

She bit her lip and nervously fingered the edge of her well-worn blouse. How strange it felt to be standing here again; the same sand, the same ocean waters, the same distant horizon, but she had been transformed.

It feels like yesterday that I stood here in this very spot, never wanting to leave home. And then we sailed away. I am Anod, the drifted one. But here I am again. Home. I'm back on Suluan. I made it. I'm alive. Everywhere I look I see my old life. But I'm not that girl anymore. I've changed. Like this great ocean without end, my life stretches out before me. I'm not afraid of leaving, or of change, or of… ever feeling lost again.

A spark of understanding flickered in Antonia's chest. She took a deep breath, trying to rid her chest of tightness. She rubbed her eyes and again breathed in the humid Suluan air. She sighed.

I'm going back inside to Mama.

All that day Antonia and Pedro went from house to house visiting her relatives and neighbors who had been left waiting the day before. She repeated her adventure story at sea over and over until she had no voice left to speak.

Papa Beni and Mam Salud graciously invited Pedro to stay in their home and sleep in Carlo's bed. Most of the friends who had traveled to Suluan from Dinagat had found a place to sleep on the island, and those who didn't fashioned make-shift beds for themselves on Pedro's big ship parked at the shoreline.

That evening Antonia came home at dusk and enjoyed the quiet peace of her home after supper. The kerosene lamp cast a warm and sleepy glow on the dingy walls covered with hand-made weavings from her mother and carved wooden bowls from her father. Looking around the dimly lit room, Antonia felt strangely detached from her former life on Suluan.

A moist breeze blew through the open windows and stars twinkled in the black fabric of the sky. She drew her feet up and wrapped her arms around her knees.

Antonia studied her mother's worn face, watching it light up with a special look that always crept over her features when she spoke to Bonifacio. Tonight's conversation with her parents and siblings focused on her upcoming wedding.

The couple would marry in the Catholic Church in Guiuan. How strange, Antonia mused. This was the plan for Carlo and Daisy, not me. Her thoughts darted back to Carlo's farewell as he swam away through the stormy waters to find help after the shipwreck.

She braced herself and leaned her chin on top of her knees, trying to keep her teeth from chattering. These memories of Carlo would haunt her for years to come, despite the happiness that she had found with Pedro. For a long while, she sat still in her own world of silence mixed with joy and sadness.

SULUAN

He's gone. Carlo is gone. Now I'm the one going to Guiuan to marry. The wedding bells will ring for me.

Her mother's simple off-white wedding dress hung on a hanger hooked over the door frame at the back of the house. Macaria had sown it by hand years ago and it fit Antonia perfectly.

The wedding in the small Catholic chapel in the town center of Guiuan was a joyful occasion not only for Antonia's immediate family who arrived for the early morning mass, but also for Pedro's entourage of friends who sailed with him from Suluan to Guiuan on his big ship.

The commotion in town perked the interest of everyone in earshot of the clanging chapel bells. Many of Antonia's Guiuan classmates curiously peered through the windows with the hope of catching a glimpse of the beautiful bride who now stood poised in the aisle of the church like an elegant dancer, strong and willowy, holding onto the arm of her father.

Her short-cropped hair was crowned with a ring of tiny florets that had been woven together by her mother early that morning. Rumors of Antonia's disappearance during the typhoon had swept through the region and seeing her now, about to wed a handsome older man, fueled the talk in town.

However, when the elderly parish priest met alone with the couple before the mass, he was quick to express his displeasure in Pedro when he failed to pray a flawless Hail Mary from memory. Pedro shrugged off the critique and spoke a heartfelt apology in perfect Waray-Waray, which unwrinkled the brow of the priest and put a smile back on his stern face.

The ceremony was simply done. In less than one half

hour, Antonia emerged from the ancient-looking whitewashed building as Mrs. Pedro Sayson. Antonia's mother's smile had been stronger that morning.

Bright, like the morning sunshine in a clear blue sky. Maybe Macaria finally overcame her worry-wart weakness. Maybe she realized on that morning that her God really does send help in time of need.

Her papa, on the other hand, had been somber, like a dark sky trying to push away thunderclouds filled with rain. He was sad to see his little girl leave home, and the pain of another separation hit him hard as they landed on the shores of Guiuan. He wasn't the only one.

But upon their return to Suluan, the festivities that welcomed them home erased any sadness that had crept into this most happy day.

The pungent aroma of roasting lechon met them at the shore. Papa Beni had slaughtered several of his prize goats and big black pots of caldereta stew were boiling over open fires around the village.

During the morning hours when the Arceno family was gone, busy housewives and many extra hands prepared for a celebration, the likes of which had never been seen before on Suluan.

Cheers and wild applause greeted the newlywed couple as they slowly walked down the plank from the big ship onto the sandy beach. Mounds of young baby coconut lay next to more sooty pots of steaming rice and cooked cassava.

The tree tops of the lanky palm trees encircling the village swayed rhythmically in the gentle breezes that blew that day. Even the trees' long green leafy hands seemed to clap together in praise and thanksgiving.

Bonifacio looked squarely in the face of his daughter-bride and cleared his throat. A faint wind rustled the palm leaves in the jungle brush behind him. Sweat trickled down his back under the hot sun, a cool breeze flowed over his wet skin.

The hour long hike up hill through the jungle to the cliffs and the cave was strenuous for everyone who joined the wedding party. Bonifacio cleared his throat again and a hush fell over those gathered at the edge of the cliff.

There in the brightness of the sun, surrounded by warmth and the cawing sound of the native birds' cheery songs, he began in a quiet voice.

"I am very proud of my girl. Tonya, your ma and I want to let you know that we never lost hope when you disappeared. We are so thankful that you kept going after the storm – past being tired – past being hungry and frightened. Past being alone. The Lord gave you hope and determination to survive and now you are alive and here today.

You are now a married young woman and the wife of a handsome sailing man. So we have come up to this place today to pay our respects to these wonderful young people, your friends, who lost their lives because of the storm.

Before you and Pedro head back to Dinagat, I thought coming up to the cave would be a good place to say our 'goodbyes'."

No one moved. Antonia blinked back tears and found it hard to swallow.

"Sir, may I also share something about your daughter?" asked Pedro.

"Of course, my son," said Bonifacio.

"Anod, just being here with you now, I feel your loss. I see the love you have for your family and for everyone on Suluan. I'm shocked to see how far the storm, the currents, and the whale shark carried you to reach the shores of Dinagat. Just looking out across the ocean from here… it is amazing to think you traveled over these great waters all alone.

I think you are the bravest, strongest girl that I have ever met, and I know that God brought you into my life. And in some strange way, I know that He will use this terrible experience to bless your life and the lives of the people on this island."

Antonia's cheeks burned.

"Will you all excuse me for a moment?" Antonia asked meekly.

She hoisted her long dress and walked carefully away from the edge of the cliff.

Antonia disappeared into the cave. The unearthly beauty of the cavern made her breathe lightly and tiptoe as she went. The dank air chilled her after the sunshine of the late afternoon. The whistling moan of the wind was loud all around her.

The pale off-white fabric of her mother's wedding dress now dragged along the pebbled ground. Powdery dust from old seashells lined the floor, and rocks of every size and shape were strewn across it. It was just as she remembered.

She glanced back at the mouth of the cave and the bright light from outside where her family and friends stood waiting. Antonia closed her eyes and swallowed hard. Her breath echoed in her ears.

She toyed with the idea of kneeling down where she and her friends had shared their last meal together, but the voice of reason whispered in her mind,

They are gone now – just hold them dear in your heart. No need to live in the past. A new life has begun.

Antonia shivered. She'd be fine. What she was leaving behind, she didn't know for sure, but one thing was certain – she was visiting her past and her future together at this very moment.

She just needed to find a memory, something she could take from this sacred place of beginnings as a symbol of her youth. Heart thumping against her ribs, she bowed down and began her search.

Little more than five minutes later, she returned to the edge of the cliff, smiling. For now, it was a delicious feeling to have returned to this place of beginnings. She stared up at Pedro, stretched out her arms and opened clenched fists full of smooth stones.

Fourteen smooth stones, seven in each hand, all about the same size and color. Antonia laid the stones carefully at the edge of the cliff and turned to the people gathered about her.

At that moment, she was reminded of the dream she had a few nights ago. She had been standing here, at this very spot, dressed in white, throwing something off of the cliff. Now it all made sense.

Antonia looked around at the people she loved most. Her parents stood together. Her siblings stood together. Mam Salud and Beni stood together. The parents of her deceased friends stood together. And she stood tall before them all with Pedro at her side. A bittersweet feeling washed over her.

We've gathered together to come up to this cave and these cliffs. Tonight we'll all go home to our own homes, but we will be forever joined in our hearts no matter how far apart we are or where we live.

"I would like to pay my respects to my fourteen friends who lost their lives in that terrible storm. Please join me in thanking God for their lives and their friendship."

There was a spattering of amens in answer.

Antonia bent down and, one by one, picked up a smooth stone and threw it from the cliff.

As she did, she loudly called out each name: "Ofelia.

Perla. Lita. Bevs".

She paused to collect herself and calm her trembling voice.

"Rey. Jhun. Amado. Peter. Roger. Mario. Alfredo. Doming".

Then she paused again and turned to smile at Mam Salud and dear Papa Beni. She stooped to picked up two stones together and then threw them high and far, and shouted the names of Carlo and Daisy. She bowed her head and stood still.

"Oh Tonya," Mam Salud whispered, "This was beautiful! Thank you. Thank you from all of us parents."

She reached out and pulled Antonia close to her oversized chest and gave her a long squeeze. Antonia looked up and saw the longing glance she gave to Papa Beni. Salud's bushy eyebrows came down momentarily.

"You know it's hard to let you go again; you've been like my own little girl since you were born."

Antonia couldn't think of anything to say.

"I will miss you dearly, Ate Salud," Antonia said, picturing Carlo's handsome face before her. "You will always be my family and I'll make sure we come home often to visit."

She lifted Salud's plump brown hand and touched it to her own forehead. She walked over to Papa Beni and did the same and then continued with each parent of her deceased friends. Her mother was waiting with open arms after she finished walking around the circle.

Antonia woke on the day of her departure and listened to the rain gently tapping on the roof. She could hear Pedro, her brothers, and her father's muffled voices downstairs.

As the party from Dinagat boarded the big ship, the sky began to clear. During the last half hour or so, the drizzle stopped. Little boys and girls darted in and out among groups of people, playing tag. The crabs along the shoreline darted in and out of their secret holes, to avoid being trampled by little feet.

The women of Suluan gathered affectionately around Macaria, while off to one side, a group of dark-skinned fishermen stood alongside Bonifacio, arms folded, surveying the big double-sail ship parked on their shores.

Mam Salud, Papa Beni, Osting, Ofelia and Perla's parents, all came with teary eyes, armloads of left-over food from the wedding reception, and jugs of fresh drinking water for the long trip.

Everyone unconsciously glanced across the heavens to make sure there were no signs of dark clouds of any size in any corner of the sky.

They had learned their lesson.

"Enjoy your sailboat ride today, and be my strong girl. Now go, write your own story," whispered Macaria into the air, as she flashed her crooked smile and then blew her daughter a kiss from the water's edge.

As the large sails billowed and caught a gust of wind, the ship was launched and slowly began its trip south to Dinagat. Antonia stood at the rail and leaned hard into the wind, waving good-bye to her family, her friends, and her beloved Suluan.

She saw little Rosalyn, the youngest sister of her cousin Lita, jumping up and down at the shore. In her hand was the small necklace that Antonia had made for her from tiny shells she had gathered the day before from the floor of the cave.

Simultaneously, Antonia pulled at the shark's tooth necklace still hanging from her own neck, and waved happily back at Rosalyn.

"Bye little Rosie, be brave and strong."

THE JOURNEY FROM SULUAN TO DINAGAT

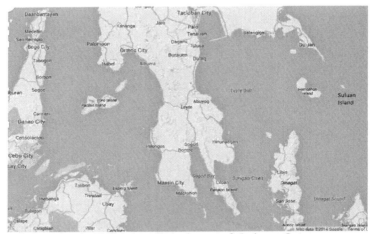

Suluan Island, Philippines (southeast of Guiuan, Samar, east
of Homonhon Island, and northeast of Dinagat Island)

DISCUSSION QUESTIONS

Dive in deeper to SULUAN and use the questions from each chapter to chat with your family or friends about the characters and themes in the book:

1) Strange superstitions and traditions haunted the cave and the cliffs of Suluan
   A. Does your family hold to any unusual beliefs or tales that have been passed down to you?
   B. How have those stories brought you fears which have affected your life?
   C. Do you have a secret "get away" place where you can go for refuge? Explain.
   D. What foreshadowing of the tragedy and return to Suluan do you find in chapters one, two, and three?

2) Childhood friends play a big role in our lives, and often memories of them linger into adulthood.
   A. Share about some of your fondest friendships and adventures from your younger years.
   B. Do you have a close friend who is opposite to your personality, but yet you still get along?
   C. Did you ever have a teenage crush? How did you get over it?

3) The race up the 490 steps to the lighthouse and the antics up at top were all fun and games.
   A. How do you feel about competition amongst

close friends?

B. Do you have memories of fighting with your siblings? Tell a story about it.

C. The tale of Magellan and his sailors impacted the boys. Has some specific event in history made a big impression on you growing up?

4) Discussion of the wedding inside the cave took many a turn.

A. Did you ever battle jealousy when another married before you? What were your struggles?

B. Daisy was a bit of an outsider on Suluan. Have you ever felt "outside" of the group? Explain.

C. What advice, if any, do you give singles who are struggling with not being married?

5) Many people hold precious memories of their hometown.

A. How would you describe the town/village/city where you grew up?

B. What are your favorite memories?

C. Have you ever felt trapped (either where you lived, or in a relationship, or in a job)? Explain.

6) Half-way to Guiuan, the sailboat met with an unexpected "monster" storm at sea.

A. Have your travel plans ever been delayed or destroyed? Share an instance where they were.

B. Antonia ignored a "sign" and a premonition before they sailed. Have you ever had such an experience?

C. What were some of Antonia's inner struggles as the boat travelled to Guiuan?

D. Do you consider the choice the boys made to swim for help a wise one? Explain.

7) The storm ripped apart the boat and the friendships of the Suluan teens.

A. How do you and people you know survive

"the storms of life"? What is your secret?

B. Have you ever rescued a friend? (*It need not be as they were drowning*) Explain the situation.

C. Say something about heroes. What qualities do you find in Carlo that made him a hero?

8) The boys gave all they could to rescue the girls.

A. Do their efforts remind you of anyone or any particular situation?

B. What must have been their thoughts as they swam through the storm?

C. Describe a time when you had to battle through something to bring help to another person or people.

9) Returning to Suluan, the parents of the boys were at a loss of what to do.

A. Mam Salud was a voice of strength in the group. Describe this woman's personality.

B. How do we cope with emergencies and tragic situations? What have you found that has helped you in perilous times in your life?

C. The small community of Suluan was close-knit. Was that a help or a hindrance during this difficult time? Explain with examples. Do you have a close-knit community around you?

10) The strong currents pulled the helpless girlfriends out to the deepest part of the Pacific Ocean.

A. How hard must it have been for Antonia to watch the demise of each of her friends?

B. Describe the fear that one would face in the deepest ocean, by day and by night.

C. How about you? Can you imagine yourself as Antonia, being lost at sea? Your reactions?

11) The death of her best friend Bevs and the shark attack are hard to fathom, let alone the arrival of a gargantuan whale shark.

A. Could you have spent the night with a corpse floating next to you as Antonia did?

B. Did Antonia take too big of a risk in mounting the whale shark?

C. Does this story remind you of another true story, fable, or legend?

12) As Antonia arrived on the shores of Dinagat, she did not realize where she landed.

A. Do you have any idea where Suluan and Dinagat are on the world map? Can you find them?

B. What are your thoughts about understanding another culture or language?

C. Agatha often wondered if God brought Antonia into their lives. What are your thoughts about this now that you have finished the book?

13) The Narciso family of six warmly welcomed this struggling teen who was on the brink of death.

A. Do you think you would have taken this risk? Why or why not?

B. What might have been some of the other problems they encountered in nursing Antonia back to health?

14) As Antonia first spoke to Pedro, he said that her healing had begun.

A. What other signs do you recall that showed the reader that Antonia was beginning to heal?

B. Talk about the term "survivor guilt". What does this mean and how do we see it in the story?

C. Healing needs to often take place on many levels. Discuss this.

15) The families back on Suluan had to come to grips with the loss of young lives.

A. What were the struggles of the boys and their parents? How difficult is it to lose a child?

B. How could this have affected the lives of others on the entire island?

C. How have you, your family, your church, or your community dealt with grief?

16) The recovery of Antonia came in stages – every member of the Sayson family was involved.

A. How would you describe the character of Bibay, Pedro's finance?

B. Why do you think Pedro struggled with his relationships with Bibay and Antonia?

C. After a typhoon, fire, or flood, how have you (or others) sped up the recovery?

17) The comical plan of Agatha and Pilar backfired, or did it?

A. Have you ever tried to match-make? Has anyone ever tried to match-make you?

B. Should we try to help others if they just don't seem to "get it" or see the relationship potential before them?

C. What about speaking up when a relationship is not healthy (as it was with Bibay)? Shall we speak up or hold our tongue?

18) The discovery of the love notes convinced Antonia that Pedro was in love with her.

A. Share a time when you wrote a love-note? If not, why not? If so, how was it received?

B. What characteristics in Antonia made her so endearing to the family?

19) Returning home to Suluan was a triumphant re-entry for Antonia. Or was it?

A. What were her fears?

B. How must have the parents of the lost children felt upon seeing Antonia alive?

C. How many years do you think it took Antonia to "get over" this tragedy? Or did she?

20) Everyone loves a happy ending, and Suluan ends on a very positive note.

A. Would you have married Pedro so quickly or spent more time back at home on Suluan?

B. Does this story seem believable? Why or why not?

C. How will you remember Antonia?

D. What life-lessons will you take with you from Suluan?

THE EPILOGUE

As told to Nancy Lueckhof by Narciso (Jhun) Sayson,
the son of Pedro and Antonia

After their marriage on the island of Guiuan and a joyful reception on Suluan, my parents, Mr. and Mrs. Pedro Sayson, settled down in Quezon, Albor, in Surigao del Norte. Papa continued with his business of selling mangrove wood, and Mama enjoyed life as a mother and housewife. Together my parents raised eleven children; two died very young.

Bienvenido (Bening) deceased ~ Rodulfo (Rudy)
Roger – deceased ~ Eduardo (Dodong)
Menrietta (Nene) ~ Narciso, Jr. (Jhun)
Virginia (Virgin) deceased ~ Berlita (Berly) deceased
Glenna – deceased at age 4
Carmela – deceased at age 3 ~ Jill

With a house full of children, one can imagine that my mother's days were filled with work. As a wife, she helped Papa in so many ways. She accompanied him to their farm and helped him plant root crops, as well as corn and rice.

Since she had overcome her fear of the sea, she often went with Papa to catch fish. I remember her as a very clever homemaker; she wove mats, cooked rice cakes and other delicacies, and sold them to help our family's finances.

Whether working in the house, on the farm, or out at sea, Mama often spiced up the day with her songs -- as she loved singing! Every morning, my mother led us in a devotional. She taught us to seek God first, before beginning our day.

Bonifacio (Antonia's father) lived out his days on the island of Suluan as a big, strapping man. He died at the ripe age of 120 years old.

Our beloved Mama passed away in our home at the age of sixty on August 4, 1982, three weeks after she underwent an operation to remove an ovarian tumor in the district hospital of Albor. After her death, Papa, my sister Jill, and I were the only ones left in our house.

Papa died in our home of unknown causes in March of 1993 in Quezon, Albor, Surigao del Norte.

Throughout Mama's life, people would regularly stop by our home and ask her to recount her extraordinary whale shark rescue story and the tale of how the Sayson family nursed her back to life. We never tired of hearing that amazing, miraculous story.

Narciso (Jhun) Sayson, son of Antonia Arceno Sayson, with his wife Beverly Ortega Sayson

WHALE SHARKS

As the largest fish in the sea, reaching lengths of 40 feet (12 meters) or more, whale sharks favorite meal is plankton. The whale shark's flattened head sports a blunt snout above its mouth with short barbels protruding from its nostrils. Its back and sides are gray to brown with white spots among pale vertical and horizontal stripes, and its belly is white. Its two dorsal fins are set rearward on its body, which ends in a large dual-lobbed caudal fin (or tail).

The above picture taken at Georgia Aquarium pictures one of the two resident male whale sharks.

TYPHOON HAIYAN

On November 8, 2013, one of history's most deadly typhoons hit the Philippines. Typhoon Haiyan, also known as Yolanda, was recorded with winds between 230-350 km/h (145-195 mph), unofficially making this storm the strongest tropical cyclone ever observed based on wind speed.

The cyclone caused catastrophic destruction in the Visayas, particularly on the islands of Samar and Leyte. The government reports that 6,500 people were killed, and countless others are still missing. Many of those who survived were left homeless. Altogether, another estimated 16.1 million people were affected.

The eye of this cyclone made its first landfall on Antonia's birthplace, the island of Suluan, in Eastern Samar. Although no one was killed, the violent winds and heavy rain left the island in total ruins.

The storm either stripped the tops off the coconut trees or tore the trees completely out of the ground. The handful of homes that were not shattered, were left severely damaged. Fishing boats were torn to shreds and scattered like toothpicks along the sandy shoreline.

The 450 families on Suluan were left with nothing but the clothes on their backs. Yolanda brought international attention from around the world, including many humanitarian agencies and NGOs. However, because Suluan is so remote, the island was virtually forgotten.

Efforts to bring relief aid went to Tacloban and Guiuan, but no one reached out to tiny Suluan.

Shortly after the storm, Friederich Lueckhof (Christian Frontier Ministries and IGC Foundation SE Asia), a close friend of Jhun Sayson, landed on the shores of Suluan with a small team through the assistance of the Philippine Navy to bring much-needed food and hygiene articles.

Since that initial trip to bring Suluan aid, Christian Frontier Ministries and IGC Foundation SE Asia have both continued to provide ongoing help in the form of new homes and fishing boats with motors to help the fishermen re-establish their livelihood. Through the help of donations from friends and partners, these ministries have committed to completely rebuild Suluan.

Antonia experienced her miraculous whale-shark rescue on the thirteenth day after an unexpected storm at sea. Now, 77 years later, because she lived and raised a caring family, help has arrived on Suluan in her darkest hour after a most terrible typhoon.

Could it be that Almighty God, in His incredible omniscience and provision, knew that through the whale-shark rescue of a fifteen-year-old girl in 1937, help would someday come to her island through one of her own children and his closest friend? He certainly is a God who is "a very present help in time of trouble". (Psalm 46:1)

Arrival with relief goods to the once beautiful shores
of Suluan shortly after typhoon Haiyan struck

Children of Suluan in front of their destroyed homes

Hundreds of Suluan homes and fishing boats in horrific ruins

Suluan ripped to shreds by Haiyan's ferocious winds in 2012

Newly built homes and motorized fishing boats from CFM

Above: Benjamin, Nancy, and Friederich Lueckhof
in the cave on the cliffs of Suluan
on their first visit to the island in 2006.
Below: Friederich in the cave in 2014

ABOUT THE AUTHOR

Nancy Stepanek Lueckhof was born in Mt. Prospect, Illinois – a charming small Midwestern suburb outside of Chicago. She received her B.S. degree in Art Therapy from William Woods University in Fulton, Missouri.

After college, Nancy taught second grade at Grace Christian School in St. Louis and later met and married the love of her life, Friederich Lueckhof, an adventurous German, who was serving as a missionary in the Philippines. She joined him there and the rest is history.

The Lueckhofs have been active in mission work in the Philippines islands for almost three decades, recently moving back to Asia after serving on the pastoral staff at the Gospel Forum in Stuttgart, Germany. The Lueckhofs have one son, Benjamin, whom they home school.

Nancy and her husband serve as the Founders of Christian Frontier Ministries, and Field Directors for IGC Foundation SE Asia in Cebu City, Philippines. A huge focus of their work, is overseeing the ministry of Pro.Vision Kids, which regularly feeds and educates over 750 slum kids around the city of Cebu and Zamboanga City with Pastors Carlo and Daisy Benitez.

When Jhun Sayson shared the phenomenal story of his mother and her miraculous whale shark rescue, as well as the humorous match-making attempts that brought his parents together, Nancy felt inspired to write SULUAN.

Her ultimate dream is to see this hard-to-believe-tale

brought to life in an animated musical film. She is currently writing a child's version of the story. The Lueckhofs have visited the island of Suluan many times and have a deep love for the people there.

Nancy is a devoted follower of Jesus Christ, and demonstrates her love to Him by serving the poor. She deeply enjoys studying and teaching the Bible, and also loves to stay fit by eating healthy, running, and laughing a lot. Nancy lives an adventurous life with her family in Talisay City, Cebu, Philippines.

Author Nancy Lueckhof at home on the island of Cebu

*SULUAN will be available in 2015 in the German language and in a soon-to-be-released children's version.

CHRISTIAN FRONTIER MINISTRIES

Friederich & Nancy Lueckhof are the founders of CFM, a non-profit Christian organization in the Philippines whose work includes discipleship, church planting, leadership training, social & medical help to the poor, disaster relief, and reaching unreached areas with the Gospel. To support the on-going relief efforts on Suluan, Pro.Vision Kids, and other valuable projects, or for more info about the work of CFM, contact Nancy Lueckhof at: n.lueckhof@gmx.de

www. cfm-network.org
Facebook: Christian Frontier Ministries
and Facebook: Pro.Vision Kids
SULUAN blog: http://suluan.tumblr.com/
Order more copies of SULUAN:
www.createspace.com/Suluan/5065405

Introducing the inspiring "You Give Me Hope" CD. Listen to the tender voices of children from the Cebu City landfill as CFM's Pro.Vision Kids sing five original songs, written especially for them by German singer-songwriter, Josua Nilkens. All proceeds from this CD go to feed and educate children in the slum areas of the Philippines. Changing the world, one child at a time! Now available on iTunes

Made in the USA
Columbia, SC
13 May 2019